I0673216

Морозко

FROST!

*Twenty Gripping
Russian Folk Tales
Retold with All of Their
Intensity and Charm*

with Imbedded Student Challenge

by

GUY GRAYBILL

FROST!

Copyright © 2012 by Guy Graybill.
Cover copyright © 2012 by Sunbury Press, Inc.

For information about special discounts for bulk purchases, please contact Sunbury Press, Inc. Wholesale Dept. at (717) 254-7274 or orders@sunburypress.com.

To request one of our authors for speaking engagements or book signings, please contact Sunbury Press, Inc. Publicity Dept. at publicity@sunburypress.com.

FIRST SUNBURY PRESS EDITION
Printed in the United States of America
November 2012

Trade paperback ISBN: 978-1-62006-098-8
Mobipocket format (Kindle) ISBN: 978-1-62006-099-5
ePub format (Nook) ISBN: 978-1-62006-100-8

Published by:
Sunbury Press
Mechanicsburg, PA
www.sunburypress.com

Mechanicsburg, Pennsylvania   USA

DEDICATION

In order to live in North America, many Russians left a rich and ancient culture. Today, they help to enrich two young and callow nations. To them, we gratefully dedicate this book.

I wish to express special thanks to Valentina Nikolaevna Golenko and her husband, Dr. Sergei Nikitich Khrushchev, for their splendid support in reading the manuscript and for suggesting several corrections that needed to be made.

ALSO BY GUY GRAYBILL

Keystone: A History of Pennsylvania ~ 2004

Explore Our Past: Elementary Level PA History ~ 2006

BRAVO!: Italian Musical Mastery ~ 2008

Prohibition's Prince: America's Millionaire Moonshiner ~ 2010

Prince & The Paupers: Companion to Prohibition's Prince ~ 2011

CONTENTS

AUTHOR'S INTRODUCTION

A skazka is a Russian folk tale. Since folk tales travel, as do the people who tell them, a skazka may or may not have originated in Russia. Also, because they were originally passed by word-of- mouth, as they were remembered, there are about as many versions of each story as there are story tellers. This means that each folk tale, before it found a permanent form in some anthology, had countless versions and variations. The story of Cinderella (or 'little cinder girl'), for example, has literally hundreds of known versions.

While many skazkas (or skazki, the Russian plural form) surely originated in old Russia, others arrived in Russia from Eastern Asia, India, Greece and elsewhere, to be modified and 'Russianized' before moving on. As they traveled, they changed to reflect the culture of their new surroundings. Still, the important story elements would remain. It is the basic element of a folk tale that would be pilfered by a Hans Christian Anderson, a Wilhelm or Jacob Grimm or a Washington Irving. Also, Russian folk tales have a gruesome characteristic that Western European and American folklorists have softened.

Our ancestors seem to have combated their deepest fears by memorializing them in their folklore. The skazka is no different, so we read of forbidden forests, ghosts, wolves, witches and demons. Also, folktales have given us some of the most familiar names in the entire human experience, from Gilgamesh and Galahad to Cinderella, the Cyclopes and Ichabod Crane.

Skazkas, or folk tales generally, gave voice to the common people, who told simple stories. Yet, these

1

tales may pleasantly surprise a modern reader, who thinks of himself or herself as being too sophisticated for such unpolished literature. The telling and retelling of these simple tales, as well as their collecting and publishing, are evidence that we adults are drawn to these tales with a fascination that matches that of younger folk.

Further proof of their appeal to adults can be found in the world of music. Some of the world's most renowned composers have placed folktales on musical pedestals. Such works would include *Billy the Kid* (Aaron Copland, 1938), *Hansel and Gretel* (Engelbert Humperdinck, the German composer; not the English counterfeit, 1893), *Cinderella* (set to music by various composers, including Rossini,1817, and Massanet, 1899), *Peter and the Wolf* (Prokofiev, 1936) and, of course, *The Nutcracker and the Mouse King* (transformed into one of the most popular of ballets, *The Nutcracker Suite*, by Peter Ilich Tchaikovsky in 1892). Lastly, it was a Russian folk tale that brought together the talents of two of Russia's artistic giants. In 1834 the noted writer, Alexander Pushkin, wrote a poem called "The Tale of the Golden Rooster." This poem became the basis of "Coq d'Or," an opera by Nicholai Rimsky-Korsakov (1907).

In addition, the adult market was certainly targeted by the Hollywood studios of the Disney animators who used folk tales for such film hits as *Snow White* (1938), *Cinderella* (1950), *Peter and the Wolf* (1946), *The Little Mermaid* (1989), and others.

My objective here was to develop a cycle of Russian folk tales that are freshly written, while conveying the essential plots and the Russian cultural settings of their 19th century versions. The basic work on which I relied for inspiration was the undated Russian Fairy Tales, collected and translated by W.R.S. Ralston and published by

Hurst and Company of New York, apparently during the 1870s. Mr. Ralston lists his principal source as being the works offered by Russian folklorist Alexander Afanasief. Sadly, Afanasief is an unfamiliar name to Americans, perhaps because names like Anderson and Grimm are so much more familiar than that of Afanasief.

In order to allow the reader the full literary impact of each tale, scenes familiar to non-Russian readers will not be pinpointed beforehand. We will only say that the reader of the following twenty skazkas may expect to recognize familiar elements from *Jack and the Bean Stalk*, *The Odyssey*, *Rip Van Winkle*, *Hansel and Gretel*, *Cinderella*, and the Biblical story of Jacob and Esau. Except for such recurring elements, the enclosed tales may be unfamiliar to American readers.

Middleburg, PA , 2012

The First Skazka

ILYA AND THE WOLF PACK

As every Russian knows, St. George has a close relationship with the wolves. He is their protector and they do his bidding. In truth, Russian wolves are known as the Dogs of St. George. This relationship was surely known to Ilya, a trapper who lived near the Vyatka River. Unlike his brother Leonid, the wealthy merchant, Ilya was poor and was often hungry as a webless spider.

The impoverished Ilya was a bachelor, having once decided that he was too poor to take a bride. His life was spent tending a lengthy trapping line that stretched along several forest streams in the region. Although he caught some animals in his iron traps, he rarely earned more than a few kopecks for their pelts.

However, it happened that one icy winter evening he set out to check his traps. He carried a gun, a knife, an empty cloth sack for the pelts and a pouch containing a crust of bread and a flask of kvass, a fermented beverage made from stale rye bread. While walking through the thick-crusted snow, he heard loud yelping, which grew louder and louder. He knew the source of the frightening sounds; a wolf pack was moving along the stream and would soon arrive where he was stopped to listen. He was too far from his village to get there before the wolves would overtake him and he knew that he might easily kill one of the pack with his weapons. However, if the wolves were ravenously hungry, as they seemed to be, the remainder of the pack could easily devour him!

Ilya was chilled by a terror that was far colder than the wintry air. He looked about. He saw a tall spruce tree with evenly-spaced branches. He quickly climbed to the top of the tree, with snow falling from the branches as he ascended. Ilya then looked beneath the tree.

The wolves were now directly below. They walked in circles beneath the very tree on which Ilya had taken refuge! They continued to howl and yelp as they sniffed the ground. Suddenly, the wolves stopped walking. They also stopped howling and yelping. Ilya was mystified.

Soon he saw two men approaching. He watched closely, still mystified. Finally, he realized that the one man, in a knight's full uniform, was St. George. The other man would be St. George's servant. Ilya could hear St. George speaking gently to the lupine beasts. They softly whimpered in reply. Then St. George turned to his servant.

"Hand me bread to feed my sharp-toothed friends."

Before answering, the servant examined the large pouch which he had been carrying.

"I'm sorry, Father; but we gave our remaining bread to the last pack of wolves that we fed."

St. George was upset.

"My servant," he admonished," you have failed me. You know that I need at least a morsel of bread for each pack that we visit!"

The servant hung his head. The saint stood in silence, looking very gloomy. The wolves whimpered more loudly...

"Father," called Ilya to St. George.

St. George looked about among the trees, not knowing where the voice originated.

Ilya shouted louder: "St. George!"

This time St. George looked upward. He spied Ilya.

"Why, pray tell me, are you in the top of a spruce tree and why, pray tell me, do you call my name?"

Ilya answered obediently.

"Father, I shall willingly answer both of your questions. In the first place, I am in a treetop because I fear your friends, the wolves. In the second place, I called to you to offer my bread for your hungry wolves. I'm sorry that I have no more than a crust."

"Toss your bread crust to me," St. George instructed; adding, "If five loaves can feed a multitude, a crust surely will feed this pack..."

Ilya dutifully dropped the lone piece of bread. St. George lifted it from the snow. He broke it into pieces and began to toss the pieces to the wolves as Ilya watched, fascinated. The thick-coated wolves seemed to be feasting on the bread offered by the illustrious saint. As the wolves finished gorging themselves, they turned, one at a time, and walked into the forest. Soon there were no wolves to be seen. While the servant stood nearby and looked particularly contrite, St. George called to the trapper who had remained perched atop the spruce tree.

"You may come down. The wolves won't harm you in any way. Further... in return for your generosity I give you my pouch and your remaining bread; but, always store your bread in the pouch. That way, you'll never want for fresh bread."

Ilya slowly climbed from the tree. He accepted the pouch from St. George and thanked him profusely. Then he gathered his own belongings and hurried home to the village, the night growing ever colder around him.

Being especially hungry and cold, as soon as he arrived at his cottage Ilya cooked a thin broth, poured it into a bowl and added most of the bread from his pouch. After supping, he crawled onto the top of his stove, where he always made his bed on cold nights. Although the fire within was dying, the stove's exterior of heavy bricks would remain warm until long after he had fallen asleep.

As the sunrise cast its brilliant reflection across the snowy crust of the meadows, Ilya was already kindling a fire of wood chips in the stove. Facing the long, cold walk along his trap line, he decided to eat the last of the bread in the pouch. To his surprise, his nostrils were filled with the savory aroma of freshly-baked bread and he found the pouch to be overflowing with the Biblical staff-of-life!

For three days he observed that the pouch, his gift from a grateful St. George, was never less than full of bread. After the third morning, he stopped to tell his wealthy brother of his good fortune. Leonid, too, marveled as Ilya related the story of his fateful meeting with St. George and of the happy result. In fact, Leonid repeatedly asked Ilya for every detail of the late-evening encounter; a request to which Ilya obligingly responded. Then Ilya said farewell to his brother and set off to check his iron traps. Leonid, however, began to lay plans for his own visit to the forest; his own encounter with the wolves and their saintly caretaker; and his own reward for being generous.

That very afternoon, Leonid told his wife that he would be late for supper, because he had an investment to make. Then he hitched his handsomest horse to his shiny, new sleigh and drove to the bakery. With a beaming smile, he placed his order.

"Give me the finest three loaves of bread that you have!"

Upon receiving the bread he had all three loaves placed in a new cloth sack. As he paid the baker, he added,

"It is likely that this is the last bread I shall purchase from your bakery."

Leonid offered no explanation to the confused baker. He simply congratulated himself on thinking of such a prophetic thought. In fact, his prophecy was about to be fulfilled. He got back onto his sleigh and drove to the approximate location that Ilya had described to him. There, he soon found an area where the snow was widely trampled and it was around the trunk of a tall spruce tree. Leonid next found a secluded area in which to tether his horse and sleigh. Then he returned on foot to the spruce tree. Carrying his new sack and its freshly-baked contents, he climbed high into the upper branches.

Presently, he heard the yelping of a wolf pack. He could scarcely control his impatience as he waited for them to arrive below. When they finally did reach the tree, they seemed unusually restless and hungry. Their howling was especially prolonged and frightening. However, St. George and his servant were quick to arrive. St. George quietly greeted the wild canine pack before turning to his servant.

"Hand me the bread to feed my sharp-toothed friends."

Before the servant could offer St. George some of the bread, Leonid shouted from his perch.

"St. George! St. George! Here is bread for you!"

St. George easily knew the direction of the loud shouting. He looked upward at Leonid, before calling in return.

"What, pray tell me, are you doing in the top of that spruce tree and why, pray tell me, are you shouting to me?"

Leonid's response had been well rehearsed in his mind.

"Father, I shall willingly answer both of your questions. In the first place, I am on a treetop because I fear your friends, the wolves. In the second place, I called to you to offer my freshly-baked bread for your hungry wolves. I'm pleased to have three expensive loaves to give you, Father."

"Well," began St. George, "such generosity deserves a reward. I pray you, come down from the tree."

As the wealthy merchant eagerly reached the base of the tree, St. George held out a hand for the bread. Leonid handed the sack to St. George and waited, expectantly. The saintly knight opened and looked into the sack. Then he closed it again and handed it to his servant, saying, "These costly loaves will make delicious eating for you and me as we travel through the forest on this cold night. Let us move on to seek our next pack of wolves."

Then he turned and addressed the wolves which had been walking around the spruce, whimpering and waiting...

"Today, you must scavenge for your food; but leave the horse untouched!"

Suddenly apprehensive, Leonid began to follow the other two men, pleading... With that, the wolves attacked the merchant, leaving little more than bloodied bones and boots!

Soon Ilya, struggling with a heavy bag of pelts, arrived. He understood the evidence before him. He wept. At last, still filled with sadness, he began to collect Leonid's meager remains. Just as he finished gathering his brother's remains, he heard the neighing of a horse. Following the sound, he discovered Leonid's horse and sleigh. Unloosing the reins from their tether, Ilya drove from the forest and returned to the village.

There is a brief epilogue to our account. It seems that when Ilya informed Leonid's wife of her

9

husband's tragic death, she overcame her grief long enough to suggest to Ilya that there was scriptural tradition supporting the sanctity of a man marrying his brother's widow. So, leftovers from the funeral supper were served, the following day, as their wedding feast. Ilya took his bread-filled pouch and went to live with his new bride. There, he enjoyed the fine house and the marital bliss which he had never before known; but, through all his remaining days, he kept his simple tastes, his generosity, his love of fresh bread... and his fear of the Dogs of St. George.

The Second Skazka

THE ONE-EYED WITCH

There was once a blacksmith named Feodor. He lived in the tiny village of Polzow. A strong and energetic man, he boasted that he had worn out two anvils during his many years of labor. Finally wealthy enough to retire, he decided that he wanted to do something which he had never done. He wanted to see a true witch. When he expressed his wish, the old men of the village told him that witches could be found in the thick forests to the east. The old men warned him, though, that witches are always evil and very dangerous. Perhaps, thought Feodor, they are right. He dropped the plan from his mind.

A few weeks later, Feodor visited the nearby tavern and had several strong drinks with his friend, Dmitri, the village tailor. With his thinking badly impaired by too much vodka, Feodor forgot the warning of danger and invited his equally intoxicated friend to join him in finding a witch.

Off they walked to the east. They soon arrived at a dense and dark forest. Still not sober enough to be fearful, they proceeded to walk into the forest along a narrow path. Thick roots and heavy undergrowth indicated that the path was rarely used. Still, Feodor and his friend continued walking, deeper and deeper into the sylvan gloom. As daylight waned and darkness crept through the trees, the vodka's effect weakened and the two men realized that they were far from home and walking through an unfamiliar land, with no place to spend the night.

However, after another turn in the path, they spied a large cottage situated by a meadow. Walking toward the open doorway, they called to the owner; but no one came to the door. They cautiously stepped inside where an unpleasant odor let them know that sheep were also housed in the cottage. As they pondered what to do, they heard bleating which was growing louder and louder. They knew that the sheepherder and flock were arriving.

The sheepherder was a stooped old lady, blind in one eye and carrying a heavy shepherd's crook. They greeted her.

"Hello, Granny. We're far from home and would like to stay here tonight if you'll allow us."

In a chilling voice, she replied, "Very good. Then I shall have one of you for supper!"

The two men were terrified!

"You're a devil!" exclaimed Dmitri the tailor.

"You're a witch!" exclaimed Feodor the blacksmith.

"Ha, ha, ha. Yes! I'm a witch!" she cackled, placing a large, iron lock on the cottage's only door.

With her special devilish strength she overpowered the two frightened men and tied them. Then she built a roaring fire in her stove and tossed the screaming tailor into the oven!

Later, as she finished supping, she pulled a stick from the woodpile, ripped free a large splinter and settled into a thick, wooden chair to pick her teeth. She let out a great belch that rumbled through the cottage, causing the poor smithy to shudder. His clothes were wet and stinking from the fearful sweat he was losing. His heavy, sheepskin jacket only added to his misery. He could scarcely think; yet he tried and tried to figure a way to save himself from tomorrow's fate. Finally, a thought occurred.

"Granny," he managed to say, "I'm... I'm a smithy."

The one-eyed witch sat silently, still picking her teeth. Again he spoke.

"Granny. I'm a smithy."

"Well," she snapped, "What can you make?"

"Oh... anything that I'm asked to make."

Again, she was silent. Then she stared directly into his eyes with her one good eye and asked, "Can you make me another eye?"

"Why of course, Granny. I... I've made dozens."

"Alright," she barked, while untying Feodor, "You make me another eye; but, if you fail, I'll roast you in an instant!"

Feodor nervously asked her for a hammer and an awl. When she provided these tools, he asked her to again sit in her great wooden chair and wait for him to prepare. She seated herself; but her good eye followed his every move as he pushed the iron awl deep into the red embers of the stove. She continued to watch closely as he removed the hot, glowing awl from the fire and poised it near her bad eye.

"Now, Granny... you must hold very still just for an instant, while I clean the socket for your new eye."

She steadied herself and soon felt her cheek growing hotter as the awl moved nearer to her bad eye.

In a flash, Feodor shifted his aim, thrusting the glowing iron awl into her good eye! He managed to drive the awl deeper with one powerful blow of the hammer before she tore free and flung herself onto the floor, shrieking and cursing!

Feodor dropped the hot awl, ready to dash for the cottage door and try to break the lock with the hammer; but the blinded witch was already there, waiting... listening... sniffing...

The poor blacksmith cowered in the farthest corner of the cottage throughout the night, afraid that if his eyes closed for just an instant, it would be his last nap. At daybreak he finally saw her stirring. She felt her way to a cupboard and pulled out a pan of bread and a jug of mead. She bit large chunks from the bread and drank the mead directly from the jug. Poor Feodor wondered if he would ever escape. Although he had the hammer, he feared that if he neared her she might use some devilish trick to again overpower him and then make him suffer horribly.

The witch, ever alert for any movement by Feodor, finished her loaf of bread. Jug in hand, she stepped to the door. She removed the lock and opened the door slightly. The sheep began moving toward the door, anxious to get to the meadow for breakfast. The witch kept her hand in front of the open doorway, grabbing each sheep by the back, counting it aloud, and then shoving it through the door.

"Nineteen... twenty... twenty one... twenty two..."

She suddenly dropped the jug and clutched the twenty-second sheep with both hands!

"Oh, no you don't... you wretch! I have just twenty one sheep in my flock!"

She felt the twenty-second sheep just briefly before realizing her mistake. Feodor, his coat turned with the fleece-side out, had already crawled past her. He had been number seventeen! Still not understanding that one leaves 'well-enough' alone, Feodor taunted the angry witch from outside her cottage.

"Farewell, you she-devil... I hope that you never again find your lost sheep."

Her angry response rattled through the forest:

"You're not finished with me yet, smithy... You'll still be tonight's meal!"

Feodor then turned and began running along the path by the same route on which he and the hapless Dmitri had arrived. As he neared the first turn, he glanced behind so see that the witch—crook in hand—was just leaving the cottage. He also noted that she was not running; but was moving forward with a determined gait. Yet, he now felt sure that he could reach Polzow safely, simply by maintaining the pace he had already begun.

As Feodor arrived at the middle of the forest, he was exhilarated by the thought that he had seen a witch and survived to brag about it. Quickly reaching the end of a long, straight, uphill path, he paused for just a moment to catch his breath. It was at that point that he saw, just ahead, a golden-handled axe imbedded in the trunk of a stout tree. The streams of sunlight that shone through the trees caused the handle to glisten. There was no doubt that the handle was made of gold and, from the moment that he saw it, Feodor knew that he must retrieve the axe before returning to his village. He was thinking, "What a fine souvenir of my adventure," so he grabbed the axe's handle with all the strength of his blacksmith's hand and he pulled. The axe didn't budge. So, Feodor put his entire body into the task; but the golden-handled axe still wouldn't move. Then he heard shouting in the distance.

"You wretch! I told you that I'd get you and I will!"

Suddenly alarmed, Feodor looked down the long hill from which he had just come. There, at the foot of the hill, barely within hearing distance, was the pursuing witch, pressing onward and shouting curses!

"You thought that you'd escape; but you can't. You blinded me; but I can still find you. Your greed made you grab my golden axe and your stinking

15

body can be smelled an hour's walk away! You'll soon know how terrible a witch's wrath can be!"

The terrified blacksmith tried to quickly push the axe from side to side; but without success. He now understood that it had a devil's curse on it. He felt that he no longer needed a souvenir of his gruesome experience. Survival was the only souvenir he wanted. However...

As he tried to release his grip from the cursed axe, he found that his fingers were stuck to the handle! He couldn't release them. The witch who was pursuing him had somehow used an enchantment to hold him until she could overtake him! He glanced back to see her slowly gaining; now she was nearly halfway up the hill. Again she cackled, "Your stench is growing worse, smithy. In a few moments you'll know the agony of a witch's revenge!"

Every devilish syllable that struck his ears added to his determination to tear loose from the axe handle and to flee; but his fingers—under her powerful spell—were forever attached to the golden handle of an axe that was forever imbedded in a tree trunk that was forever rooted in the eternal earth! His dreaded pursuer was now just a few paces away, laughing loudly and wickedly!

Once again, desperation spurred thought. He remembered that he always carried a very sharp knife, as did all the men of the village. With his free hand he pulled his knife from its sheath. He began hacking away at his own fingers and pulling on his captive hand with all his strength.

Suddenly, the last severed finger ripped loose and he stumbled backward. In a near panic he recovered his balance and lunged down the path toward Polzow!

The demon, sensing his escape, shouted after him, "Run, you miserable rabbit! I can still smell your stinking body and I'll chase you right into your warren and drag you back to my cottage!"

Half running and half stumbling, the bloody-handed blacksmith hurried toward his village, which was still some distance away. He could hear a stream babbling somewhere to his left. Still determined to outwit and outrun the raging pursuer, Feodor ran to the stream and then ran beside it until he came to a deep, calm pool. Quickly removing all his clothing, he plunged into the chilly waters. He hastily rinsed his entire body, even submerging his sweaty head. Then, he lifted the stinking bundle that had been his clothing and laid it on the side of the pool that was more distant from the path. He quickly rinsed only his shoes and two undergarments. He slipped into his soggy shoes and the one wet undergarment before wrapping the other wet garment around the bloody stump of his hand as he walked. He was walking toward Polzow as quietly as he could.

Within a few moments, Feodor heard a splash and loud cursing. He knew that the witch had stumbled into the pool while hurrying to overtake the stench of his discarded clothes!

When he finally stumbled into Polzow, he told the villagers his harrowing story and he showed them his fingerless hand. They marveled at his account; but he never again mentioned his ordeal, nor did he ever again express any desire to see a real witch.

The Third Skazka

THE MIDNIGHT VISITOR

Many years ago, in a small Russian village, there lived a young husband and wife. They were a happy and loving couple, the envy of their neighbors. When it became known that the wife was pregnant, all the villagers shared the couples' joy in awaiting the birth of their first child. However, the joy turned to sorrow for the woman died during childbirth.

The poor husband was filled with sadness and concern. Even before his wife could be buried, he had to find a woman to help care for his motherless, newborn son. When he was told of a kindly old widow in a nearby town who might care for the infant, he quickly traveled to that village and hired the woman to come live with him and care for his son.

After a few days, the old woman told the widower father that something strange was happening. She said that the infant refused to eat or drink; but spent the entire day crying. In addition, the woman told her employer, every night the unfed baby grew quiet about midnight and seemed to sleep peacefully throughout the remainder of the night. Just as strange, the woman further related, was that for the past three nights—just as the mantle clock struck midnight—she had heard the cottage door open and soft footsteps move toward the baby's cradle!

The old woman asked, "Who could it be?" But, the poor father was just as mystified as she. Since no one in the village ever entered another person's cottage unless invited, the father told the woman that he would watch with her that very night.

Near midnight, the father lighted a candle and hid it under an earthen crock. Then he and the old woman sat on the floor near the whimpering baby and waited. Sure enough, just as the old woman had claimed, as the clock was striking 'twelve', the door latch clicked and the door squeaked open. They heard the faintest of footsteps move across the wooden planks of the cottage floor toward the cradle. The husband waited, nervously, for a few moments and then lifted the crock, uncovering the lighted candle.

They were too shocked to speak. There, kneeling beside the cradle, was the ghost of the dead mother! She was still wearing her burial clothes and she was cradling the baby in her arms and nursing it at her dead breast. The dead mother briefly looked at them with a ghastly stare, then silently and gently laid the infant in its cradle. Looking very, very sad, the dead mother slowly arose and gave a final, sorrowful glance at her poor son, before walking through the cottage door and disappearing into the night. After a minute of stunned silence, the young widower lifted the candle and he and the old woman stepped over to the cradle. Looking down, they were horrified. The baby, too, had died.

The Fourth Skazka

CROSSING THE DON

Seventeen-year-old Oleg Davidovich Donskoi, as his surname implied (Donskoi means "of the Don River"), lived near the Don River in southern Russia and he often walked the hour's walk to the river's bank in order to catch fish. As was common in old Russia, rivers were especially honored and revered. So it was with the Don. Oleg Davidovich had learned from his father, David, and from their neighbors, to pray to the Don River for good weather or good fishing. Also as his father had taught him, Oleg poured an occasional swallow of kvass, or tossed a kopeck coin, into the Don as a sacrifice.

Oleg's father, David Donskoi, had never traveled more than a half-day's journey from his home; but he had heard that the Don was one of Russia's greatest rivers and he never grew tired of telling young Oleg, "Our neighbor, the Don, is a majestic and powerful river."

One day Oleg Davidovich decided to join the tsar's imperial army. However, the regional military post was on the opposite side of the Don. In addition, the nearest bridge was two day's walk upstream. On the day of his departure, he hugged his tearful mother, his quiet father, and each of his brothers and sisters. Then, carrying a small sack of food and clothing, he walked alone to the river bank. There Oleg untied the strings of the leather purse that had been fastened to his belt. He removed three kopecks and tossed them into the flowing stream.

"Comrade River," he solicited, "I am on my way to the army camp; but the nearest span over your deep waters is two days journey to the north. Would you please show me a ford that will shorten my travels?"

A voice, deep and sonorous, arose from the depths of the Don.

"My young suppliant," the river began," there is a place four turns to the south, where tall cliffs grace my far shore. My waters there are wide but shallow. You can cross safely. Once across my ford, you will see a narrow path where wild sheep descend to drink. Follow that path to the top of the cliff and you will soon arrive at the road to your destination."

Oleg Davidovich thanked the river and proceeded along the nearer bank until he had passed four bends of the Don. Once there, he looked across the river to see cliffs; but only after he had waded the shallow, wide channel did he see the wild sheeps' path on the face of the cliff. As Oleg carefully climbed along that path it occurred to him that he might be the only person who knew of the ford. The thought pleased him immensely.

When he arrived at the military post he was formally inducted into the tsar's imperial army and was given proper military gear before going to his first army meal. While eating, his fellow soldiers casually asked the location of his home. He was quick to tell them, "I live due west, across the Don; but I didn't travel for days to a bridge. Instead, I forded the river close by."

"That's impossible," the listeners would protest. "All the fords are far upstream where the Don is but a rivulet!"

"Not for me, comrades," Oleg boasted, "I cross where I please. Everyone says that the Don is a majestic and powerful river. Ha! To me, the mighty Don is no more than a puddle!"

As the days passed, his military associates continued to question his claims. The more they marvelled, the more wildly he bragged. Typical of Oleg's version of things was his newer boast that the Don purposely froze early so that he could cross in autumn and then thawed early if he wished to fish! In truth, Oleg became fascinated with the notoriety that his claims had brought him. Even after the soldiers tired of hearing him, and stopped discussing the daunting Don, Oleg boasted.

At last the day arrived when Oleg would take his first furlough. The boastful private was eager to return home to see his family and friends. His fellow soldiers were also eager for his departure from the post in order to gain a respite from his incessant bragging! By midday, Oleg was again at the Don. He cautiously descended the wild sheep's path to the river's edge and eagerly began to wade toward the home shore.

Suddenly, the river sent an undercurrent through the shallow ford! Oleg's feet were washed from beneath him! His pack fell from his grip and began bobbing as it floated with the current. Oleg, floundering and slipping below the surface, shouted.

"Comrade River! Save me... save me!"

Washing downstream toward the deeper, swifter channel, he managed to shout another time.

"Comrade... I've three kopecks! Please spare me!"

The river answered Oleg's plea.

"Your disrespect and your boasting have decided your fate, Private. This time, I refuse your three kopecks. They will buy you just one item... a watery grave."

Most of the Don's reply went unheard by Oleg, who quickly disappeared beneath the swirling, churning waters.

Three days later, some fishermen in the Sea of Azov observed an army canteen floating on the current that empties the Don River into the ancient sea. The canteen was the only remains anyone ever found from Oleg Davidovich Donskoi, the braggart who angered the mighty Don, one of Russia's most majestic and powerful rivers.

The Fifth Skazka

TWO COMRADES

Once upon a time, oh, very long ago, there were two friends, Anton and Mikhail. They worked in a saddler's shop and spent every evening together in drinking and carousing. But, in more serious moments they created this pact of friendship: They would always be friends and when either married, he'd be certain to invite the other to the wedding.

Although the pact was simple, it became somewhat complicated a few months later when Mikhail was stricken ill with a terrible fever. As soon as Anton learned of Mikhail's malady, he hurried to visit his dearest friend; but he arrived too late. Mikhail had already died, suddenly and peacefully.

The following year, Anton began to court a young woman in the neighboring village of Karlovsk. Within a few months a wedding was planned for late July, following the Feast of St. Vladimir. Early in the morning of his wedding day, Anton and his many relatives climbed onto several horse-drawn wagons and began the trip to Karlovsk. As they arrived at the edge of their town, Anton recalled his friendship with Mikhail and the binding pact which they had made.

"Stop the wagons!" Anton shouted.

The drivers shouted orders to the horses, tugged the reins, and brought the wagons to a halt. Members of the wedding party looked at Anton, awaiting an explanation. Anton provided one.

"My good friend, Mikhail resides here, in a plot near the far corner. I promised to invite him to my

24

wedding and I will. I'll be gone for just a few moments."

With that declaration, Anton jumped from the groom's wagon to the ground and began running joyously into the sacred grounds; while in the wagons the young people laughed and joked about Anton's behavior as the elderly folks shook their heads in disapproval.

As Anton reached the corner of the churchyard, he glanced at the grave markers until he saw the stone that he had been seeking. It said:

Mikhail Vasilievich Lopatnikov
b. 1511   d. 1530
"A dutiful son, returned to his Maker"

As Anton read the sparse inscription, he became forlorn. Here were the mortal remains of a young man known to the townspeople as Mikhail Vasilievich, the son of Vasili Lopatnikov; and known to his family and to his friend, Anton, as "Mishka." Anton spoke, solemnly and softly.

"Mishka... I've come to fulfill our friendship agreement. I'm here to invite you to my wedding to drink a toast to my marriage and to my beautiful bride!" Then he added, sadly, "Now I must go, Mikhail... I must go."

Before Anton could turn on his heels to leave, the earth suddenly opened and Anton stared into Mikhail's grave! Then the lid flew from the plain, walnut casket and the ghost of Mikhail stepped out and leaped from the gaping hole onto the solid land above.

Anton, shocked by Mikhail's appearance, stepped backward; but Mikhail grabbed him by the shoulders and wrapped his ghastly arms around Anton. In a moment, Mikhail released his hold, shouting.

"Comrade! You remembered. No one has ever had a truer friend! Come, let us drink!"

Mikhail jumped back into the yawning grave. Anton, trembling from the astonishing encounter, stood transfixed for several seconds. Then he stepped closer and peered into the spectral pit. He watched, fascinated, as Mikhail lifted two cups and a bottle of dark liquor from within the open casket. Anton's ghostly comrade again summoned the prospective groom.

"Comrade, I beseech you. Join me for a drink so that we can profit from this visit."

Mikhail poured the two drinks, sat the bottle back in the casket, and raised one of the cups toward Anton.

"All right, friend. I'll have a quick toast with you; but then I must hurry back to the wedding party. My bride is waiting."

With that declaration, Anton jumped into the grave beside the ghost of his friend, Mikhail. Mikhail raised his own cup and offered a toast to the loving couple. As they drank the liquor, a score of years rolled by!

Mikhail poured two more drinks, declaring, "Have another, Comrade, so that you might offer a toast for my soul."

"Of course," Anton agreed, accepting the newly-filled cup.

"But, I really must hurry... My relatives are waiting!"

The two again raised their cups as Anton offered his toast.

"May your worthy soul elude the flames of Hell and know eternal peace!"

They drank... and another score of year passed.

Before Anton could speak again, Mikhail declared, "Well spoken, comrade; a right worthy toast. So, let us have a third and final drink. Then you may go with my full blessing!"

This time, Anton needed no coaxing; but offered his cup for a third portion of the dark liquor.

"Let the devil take them if they become impatient," Anton observed, as the cups were again filled and raised.

Mikhail offered the final toast.

"May our souls meet again in Eternity."

"May our souls meet again in Eternity," Anton agreed. Then he emptied his cup as a third score of years fell away!

As the last drop trickled down his throat, Anton said farewell to his comrade and jumped out of the grave. He turned to offer a parting salute; but at that instant the casket lid fell shut over Mikhail's corpse and the earth slowly closed over the entire grave.

Anton stood beside the closed grave and looked in every direction. He was utterly dumbfounded! There were no standing tombstones. The few that Anton saw were lying flat, nearly smothered by weeds and brambles! Overcome by confusion and anxiety, he ran toward the road where he had separated from his wedding party. He ran, stumbling, through thick briars that tore at his clothing and scratched at his flesh.

When he finally stumbled onto the road, bits of broken briars were caught in his trousers and jacket; but there was no one to be seen. Anton paused just long enough to remove the briars from his clothing. Then he began running toward Karlovsk, the village of his bride. He called to each of the several people he encountered who were traveling in the other direction.

"Have you seen a wedding party traveling toward Karlovsk?"

They all eyed Anton critically, silently shook their heads in the negative, and drove on. Only the last traveler to whom he called spoke; but only to chastise him!

"You're drunk! You're supposed to do your drinking at the wedding feast... How shameful!"

Anton continued running until he arrived, breathless, in Karlovsk. There he found that the entire main street was unfamiliar. He paused at the shop of the tanner whom he had visited several times to get leather for his employer, the saddler; but the sign above the doorway had a different shape and message: The Tsar's Crown. It was now a tavern.

Anton continued along the street until he reached the old cathedral. There was no one in the nave. He sought the priest; but it was not the same one who was to perform the marriage ceremony.

"Father," Anton blurted, "where is the wedding?"

The priest explained that there were no weddings scheduled for the day in Karlovsk. When Anton insisted that he had arrived for his own wedding, the priest gently asked him to relate all that had happened. When Anton finished his account, the priest spoke kindly.

"My son, what you witnessed in the churchyard was both evil and supernatural. Come, let us search through the old church records."

Anton followed the holy man to an alcove that contained several huge, dust-laden journals. Going from the recent to the older records, the priest finally turned a crumbling page, then paused.

"Here it is, my son. The ink is pale; but legible... and it appears that sixty years ago your wedding was scheduled here. Your wedding party arrived to say that you had disappeared in their local graveyard. The ceremony was canceled."

Anton shook his head in despair and stood in abject silence as the priest slowly turned the pages of the church's hoary history.   Again, the priest found a significant entry.

"And here... it's recorded that the bride, the following year, married a young man from right here in Karlovsk."

They say that Anton never returned to his native village. Instead, he remained in Karlovsk where he, too, entered the priesthood. Of course, priests of the Russian Church were allowed to marry; but they also say that Anton chose to remain a bachelor.

The Sixth Skazka

FROST

Stretching east to west across Russia is a vast belt of dense forest land. To its north, hard by the Arctic Ocean, lies the barren, frozen tundra while, to its south lies the immense grassy plains or steppes. It was in a village located within the great expanse of Russian forests that, many, many years ago, old Maxim lived with his second wife, his own daughter and his wife's two daughters.

Maxim's wife, Marina, doted on her two natural daughters, Prascovia and Mashka, while showering constant abuse on their older stepsister, Sofya. It was Sofya who was assigned to do all the work of the household. Before sunup she gave fodder and water to the cattle, carried water into the house, brought firewood for the great stove and swept the floors. Even then, her stepmother grumbled.

"What a lazybones you are! And such a sloppy one! Look at this! You left this hairbrush lying about. You dropped a wood chip on the door step and you even tracked mud into the house!"

The girl kept silent and cried; she tried in every way to win her stepmother's approval and to be of service to her stepsisters. However, Prascovia and Mashka, following their mother's lead, also insulted and quarreled with Sofya. If their abuse caused tears, they were even more delighted. The two sisters, of course, also slept late, bathed in water provided by Sofya, waited for Sofya to serve their dinners and made sure that Sofya found time to mend their clothing.

Old Maxim loved his daughter dearly. He was pleased that she was polite, industrious and obedient; but he was also feeble and cowered before his scolding wife and her two obstinate and lazy daughters. He simply knew of no way to help his suffering, eldest daughter. This was the situation when Sofya, Prascovia and Mashka finally reached the age for marriage.

There was but one object in the entire household that cost more than a ruble or two, the copper samovar that Sofya always kept clean and shiny. This metal urn held water for tea; water kept boiling hot by having a central tube filled with hot charcoals.

Late one night, Marina snapped at Sofya, "Look here, lazy one, draw some water and make tea for your father and me, then off to bed with you."

Maxim watched as his dutiful daughter went to the samovar, turned the spigot and drained enough hot water to fill two tea cups. After the tea and sweetener were added, Sofya served her parents and then quietly retired to her bed.

Maxim silently drank his tea, not wishing to say something to which his wife would take offense.

Marina soon turned to her husband, "I say, old man, let's get Sofya married. I've found a very eligible groom."

"If that's what you think best," he replied solemnly, not wishing to reveal his pleasure at the thought of his daughter finally escaping the sharp tongue of her stepmother. He then stood and began slinking off to his bed above the stove. Sofya called after him.

"Listen, greybeard. Get up early tomorrow and harness the mare to our sledge, so that you might take Sofya on a trip to meet the groom."

She then shouted to Sofya.

"Sofya, in the morning put your things together in a basket and put on your best clothing. Your father will be driving you to meet your handsome bridegroom!"

"Yes, Mother," came the polite reply. Sofya was delighted with the prospect of meeting her future husband and of having a house of her own to clean and tend; but a house without the harsh words of her stepmother. Both father and daughter slept comfortably through the icy winter night.

Sofya was awake and busy before daylight, quietly washing, dressing and praying. She also packed her modest belongings and looked from the window to see how soon her father would be ready for their journey.

Meanwhile, as the last stars were fading into daylight, Maxim harnessed the mare to the sledge and brought it to the steps. He noted, with inner pleasure, Sofya's smiling face as she peered through the window. He leaned, slightly, to avoid the long icicles, knowing that to knock icicles from their perch would anger Morozko [Jack Frost]. Then he went indoors and sat on the windowsill. He announced proudly:

"Well, I've got everything ready."

"Well, you needn't shout it for the whole forest to hear! There's no need to awaken poor Proscovia and Mashka. Now, then, you and Sofya sit up to table and eat your breakfast and don't be all day about it!"

Maxim moved to the table and took a seat beside Sofya. He took bread from a pan and cut some for Sofya and for himself. His wife served a helping of old cabbage soup to each, telling Sofya, "There, my pigeon. Eat and be off. I've looked at you quite enough!"

As Sofya and Maxim finished their breakfast, Marina spoke again.

"You listen carefully, old man. It's time for you to take Sofya to her bridegroom. So, drive straight down the forest road. At the first road to your right, turn off. Drive up that steep hill to the great pine that sits in the meadow on top of the ridge. You know the one. Have Sofya get off there and you come directly home. Sofya can wait there to meet her handsome bridegroom, Morozko!"

The old man's eyes opened wide. So did his mouth. Sofya began to sob. Her mother chided her.

"Stop all this fuss. Surely, your bridegroom is handsome as well as being very rich. Why, just see all that belongs to him. He owns the birches, the firs and the pines and he covers them all with robes of white fur. Morozko's wealth is the envy of everyone... and, besides, he's such a romantic figure!"

Neither Maxim nor his sweet daughter protested. He simply had her put on her heavy fur coat and they stepped outside, avoiding the icicles. Both climbed aboard the sledge. Maxim cracked the whip and they set off on their journey. Once deep in the forest, they traveled upwards over a thick-crusted snow until they reached a high meadow and the towering, snow-covered pine that stood in the center of the meadow. There Maxim helped Sofya from the sledge, handed her belongings to her and climbed back onto the sledge. Before driving home again, he told Sofya:

"Sit here and await your bridegroom. And mind you, receive him as pleasantly as you can."

"I will, dear Father," she said softly, as he turned the horse and drove toward home.

Sofya sat and shivered. Her warm coat couldn't keep out the intense cold. Her teeth chattered. Suddenly she heard a sound. Not far off, Morozko was cracking away on a fir. He leaped from fir to fir, snapping his fingers and leaving branch after branch glazed with ice. Soon he was on top of the very tree under which Sofya was sitting and shivering. He called to her.

"Are you warm, maiden?"

"Yes, I'm warm, Father Frost," answered the shivering girl.

Frost began to descend lower on the tree, all the while snapping and cracking his fingers.

"Are you warm, maiden? Are you warm, pretty one?"

Although shivering and whimpering, she managed a polite response.

"Yes... I'm warm, Father Frost. I'm warm Frost, dear."

Still he descended, fingers snapping and an icy wind now swirling around her.

"Are you warm, maiden? Are you warm, pretty one? Are you warm, my darling?"

Sofya was shivering, whimpering and cringing with the coldness that wrapped her. She could scarcely speak; but she still managed to murmur:

"Oh, yes... I'm quite warm, Frost dearest!"

Then Morozko took pity on her, wrapped her in thick furs and warmed her with heavy woolen blankets.

The next morning, Marina said to her husband:

"Well, old one... drive out and wake the young couple!"

The old man wearily harnessed his mare, climbed aboard the sledge and drove into the forest. When he arrived at the tall pine, he found that Sofya was alive and that she had been given a fine greatcoat, an expensive bridal veil, and a basket filled with rich gifts. He stowed all her belongings on the sledge, helped his daughter to climb aboard, took his seat beside her and drove home. The two rode in silence, with the intense cold unable to prevent a trace of a smile on each of their faces.

Her stepmother was stunned to see Sofya alive! She was also angered to see the fine gifts given to her stepdaughter.

"You two connivers. You can't trick me!"

However, before Maxim had even unloaded the sledge, Marina had another thought.

"Well, old man, you've got another task for tomorrow. You can take my own two beauties out to their bridegroom in the morning. Martha's gifts are nothing compared to what Morozko will give them!"

Early the next morning the old woman gave her daughters their breakfasts, dressed them in their finest outfits and sent them off on their journey. And, just as before, Maxim left them beneath the great pine.

The two sisters sat beneath the tree laughing and saying: "Whatever was Mother thinking? All of a sudden she decides to get both of us married... and just as though there were no nice lads in our village.

Goodness knows who might come along out here or how terrible he might be!"

Although dressed in very warm coats, both girls were feeling the sting of cold air.

"I say, Prascovia, this frost is getting worse. If our bridegroom doesn't soon arrive, we'll freeze to death!"

"That's nonsense, Mashka; as if suitors normally arrived in the forenoon. We've got a long wait ahead."

"But, Prascovia. What if only one groom arrives. Who will he choose?"

"Well, not you, you silly goose!"

"Oh, so I suppose that it will be you!"

"Of course, it will be me!"

Meanwhile, Morozko had numbed the girls' hands, so they stuffed their hands deeper into their clothing and continued their argument.

"You're a fright. You're the laziest! You don't even know how to begin weaving, let alone how to finish a garment!"

"You boaster! As though you know anything about anything... except being silly and eating everything in sight!"

While the girls continued to scold one another, they became truly numb with cold. Suddenly they both cried at once: "Where is my groom? Do you know that you're turning quite blue?"

Now Morozko was moving closer and sitting on the nearest tree to the one under which the freezing girls were awaiting marriage. As he moved to the top of their tree, with fingers snapping, Mashka was certain that someone was arriving.

"Listen, Prascovia! He's finally arriving, and with bells, too."

"You lie! I won't listen. My skin is peeling from the cold!"

"Well, I never heard of a bride with her skin peeling!"

Morozko, seated at the top of the very tree under which the girls suffered, called down to them.

"Are you warm, maidens? Are you warm, pretty ones? Are you warm, my darlings?"

"Oh, Frost, it's awfully cold! We nearly perished! We're waiting for a bridegroom; but the stupid fellow has disappeared!"

Morozko slid lower down the tree, snapping his fingers even faster than before.

"Are you warm, maidens? Are you warm, pretty ones?"

"Get away from us! Are you so blind that you can't see that our hands and feet are frozen?"

Edging closer to the sisters, Morozko again asked,

"Are you warm, maidens?"

"Down into the bottomless pit, with you, Frost! Curse you! Get out of our sight," they snapped as their bodies became more and more numb.

The next morning, Marina could barely wait for Maxim to depart.

"Sofya and I will have a nice big breakfast ready when you return, so just go, now, and bring back my daughters. There's a terrible frost about, so do hurry!"

When Maxim arrived at the tall pine, he found that his young stepdaughters were dead. Sadly, he lifted them onto the sledge, wrapped a blanket around them and covered them with a bark mat. While he was still a far distance from the house, the old woman saw him arriving and ran to meet him.

"Where are the girls?"

"In the sledge."

Marina lifted the mat, undid the blanket and found her frozen daughters. Staggering back from the wagon, she turned on her husband with the fury of a blizzard.

"What have you done, you wretch? You've killed my daughters! You've destroyed by beautiful, beautiful girls, my flesh and blood... my sparkling gems!"

She began shrieking threats.

"You'll learn! I'll lash you with the horsewhip! I'll thrash you with the iron poker!"

Maxim shouted, "That's enough, you old goose! You're the one who flattered yourself that you would gain riches from your ill-trained daughters. You're the one who sent two spoiled and stiff-necked maidens to try to warm old Morozko. How was I to blame? You're the one who did all the plotting here!"

For weeks Marina raged. But, as time passed, she began to appreciate her husband and her stepdaughter and they began living in a household without malice and harsh words. The following year, a neighbor made an offer of marriage. A wedding was celebrated and Sofya continued to live nearby. As Sofya bore children, her stepmother proudly showed them to the villagers. Meanwhile Maxim taught his grandchildren to be respectful and polite, while he occasionally enjoyed frightening them with stories about Morozko.

The Seventh Skazka

IVASHKA

There was once an old couple who had one son, named Ivan. No one can tell how fond they were of young Ivan, whom they affectionately called "Ivashka."

Well, one day Ivashka said to his old parents:

"I'll go fishing if you'll let me."

"Whatever are you thinking. Why, you're much too small to be fishing. Suppose you fell into the river and drowned; what good would there be to that?"

"No, no. I'll not drown. I'll be very careful, just as you've taught me! And, I'll catch you some fish. Do let me fish."

They finally accepted his assurances and agreed that he could go fishing, so his mother slipped a white shirt onto Ivashka and tied a red girdle around him and watched as he carefully climbed into their small boat. Once seated in the boat he said:

Boat, boat, float a little farther.
Boat, boat, float a little farther.

Then the boat floated farther and farther into the river as Ivashka began to fish.

After some time had passed, his old mother hobbled down to the riverbank and called to her son:

Ivashka, Ivashka, my boy,
Float up, float up unto the riverside;

I bring you food and drink.

So Ivashka said:

Boat, boat, float to the riverside;
My mother is calling to me.

The boat floated to the shore, where the woman took the fish, gave her son food and drink, changed his shirt and his girdle and sent him back to fishing. Again, as he sat in the boat Ivashka said:

Boat, boat, float a little farther,
Boat, boat, float a little farther.

Again the boat floated on farther and farther, while young Ivashka fished.

Some time later, the old man hobbled down to the bank and called to Ivashka:

Ivashka, Ivashka, my son,
Float up, float up unto the riverside.
I bring you food and drink.

Again, Ivashka commanded the boat and, again, the boat floated to shore.

The old man took the fish, gave his boy food and drink, changed Ivashka's shirt and his girdle and sent him back to his fishing.

Now it happened that a certain witch had seen all that had taken place. She decided to use a trick to capture the lad, so she went to the riverbank and cried out in her hoarse voice:

Ivashka, Ivashka my boy,
Float up, float up unto the riverside;
I bring you food and drink.

Ivashka realized that the voice was not that of his mother; but of a witch. He called to his boat:

Boat, boat, float a little farther.
Boat, boat, float a little farther;
That is not my mother; but a witch who calls.

As Ivashka's boat sailed farther from shore, the witch realized that she must call Ivashka with just such a voice as his mother's. So she rushed to a smith and declared, "Smith, smith. Make me just such a thin, little voice as Ivashka's mother has... or I'll kill you!"

About mid-afternoon the witch hurried to the river in order to be there before Ivashka's mother arrived. She quickly called, in her new voice:

Ivashka, Ivashka, my boy,
Float up, float up unto the riverbank.
I bring you food and drink.

As Ivashka's boat touched the shore, the witch grabbed his fish and grabbed Ivashka! She quickly carried the struggling boy to her home in the forest.

When the witch arrived with her captive, she said to her daughter, Elena, "Alenka, heat the stove as hot as you can. Then bake Ivashka, while I gather my friends for the feast!" Soon Alenka had the stove heated ever so hot. So she said to Ivashka, "Come here and sit on this shovel."

"I'm still very young and foolish," he answered. "Please show me what you want me to do."

"Very well," replied Alenka. "It won't take but a moment to teach you."

But, the moment that Alenka sat on the shovel, Ivashka grabbed the shovel and tossed the witch's daughter into the oven, slamming shut the oven door and running from the hut, locking the door behind him. Knowing the witch might return at any moment, Ivashka quickly climbed to the top of ever so high an oak tree.

After some time, the witch arrived with her guests. She knocked at the door of the hut; but nobody opened it for her.

"Ah! That cursed Alenka!" she cried. "She's gone away without permission again. No one is so disobedient as Alenka."

The witch proceeded to climb through a window. Then she opened the door to admit her guests. They all sat at the table while the witch opened the oven and took out the baked body. All ate their fill and drank their fill before going into the courtyard where they began dancing on the grass.

"I turn about, I dance about, having fed on Ivashka's flesh," cried the witch. "I whirl about and dance about, having fed on Ivashka's flesh."

From his perch atop the great oak, the foolish boy called down: "You turn about and dance about, having fed on Alenka's flesh!"

The witch paused. She tilted her head and listened.

"Did I hear something? It must have been the rustling of the leaves."

So the witch began again: "I whirl about and dance about, having fed on Ivashka's flesh."

Ivashka raised his youthful voice: "You whirl about and dance about, having fed on Alenka's flesh!"

This time the witch jerked her head skyward. Her face flushed crimson and her eyes turned a fiery red! Suddenly terrified, Ivashka cowered behind some leafy branches; but he was too late.

As the witch's ghoulish guests watched, the witch rushed at the tree and began gnawing on the trunk, as Ivashka shook with fright. She gnawed and gnawed until her two upper front teeth snapped off. So she rushed to the iron forge and ranted at the smith: "Smith, smith, make me some iron teeth or I'll devour you!"

So the smith forged her two iron teeth.

The witch returned and began gnawing on the oak once more. She gnawed and gnawed, until the tree began to totter, shaking Ivashka almost to the point of falling. But he saw the tree leaning closer to a second, nearby oak, so he jumped into that tree's upper branches just as the first oak crashed to the ground!

The witch shrieked in triumph when the tree fell! Then she saw that Ivashka was seated, safely, in another oak, now the only tree remaining in the area. With total spite, she loudly gnashed her teeth. Then she began to gnaw at the second tree. She gnawed and gnawed until, suddenly, her two bottom front teeth broke and fell to the ground! Again she ran to the forge.

"Smith, smith, make me two iron teeth or I'll roast you for supper!"

The smith forged two more iron teeth for her and the witch hurried back to her trembling captive. She began to gnaw the trunk of the remaining oak more vigorously than before, with wood chips flying in all directions!

With the first quiver of the tree beneath him, Ivashka looked heavenward, imploringly. Then, as his gaze fell he saw three dark lines in the sky, just above the horizon. As they grew closer, they took the shape of 'V's. Ivashka now recognized the approaching forms as flocks of birds.

He quickly called to the birds to save him.

Oh, my swans and geese,
Lift me with your strong wings.
Carry me to my father and mother,
To the cottage of my father and mother,

Where I can eat and drink in safety!

The leader of the flock called back, "Let the birds in the middle flock carry you."

Ivashka waited nervously for the second flock to fly near before shouting:

Oh, my swans and geese,
Lift me with your strong wings.
Carry me to my father and mother,
To the cottage of my father and mother
Where I can eat and drink in safety!

The leader of the second flock called back, "Let the birds in the next flock carry you."

By the time the next flock drew near, the tree was shaking violently. But, Ivashka held tight to the upper branches and managed to call once more:

Oh, my swans and geese,
Lift me with your strong wings.
Carry me to my father and mother,
To the cottage of my father and mother
Where I can eat and drink in safety!

This time several swans and geese bit firmly into Ivashka's clothing, lifting him from the oak. The upper branches of the tree whipped the escaping Ivashka as it, too, fell to the earth. The witch and her terrified guests scrambled as the heavy oak crashed onto the cottage, leaving only a heap of splinters beneath the giant trunk!

Meanwhile, the helpful swans and geese were swiftly transporting Ivashka away from the forest and to the cottage of his grieving parents. Under the starlit sky they gently dropped him onto the broad windowsill of the little window of his bedroom.

Early the next morning, Ivashka's mother began making pancakes and wailing sadly:

"Where is our darling Ivashka? Oh, if only I could see him for one last time, even if only in a dream..."

Then his father moaned, as tears flowed down his cheeks, "I dreamed that swans and geese had brought our Ivashka home."

His mother only sobbed. As the pancakes finished cooking, she said to her husband, "Here, old man. We must eat. Here's a pancake for you and here's one for me. Here's another for you, father, and here's another for me."

From the upper room, Ivashka, called softly, "Is there none for me."

"Here's another for you, father, and here's another for me," continued the distraught woman.

"And none for me?" repeated Ivashka.

"Why, old man, go and see what is making that noise in the upper room."

The father climbed into the upper room and there he found their son. The jubilant father quickly climbed down to tell his wife the good news, with Ivashka right behind him!

As the three ate their pancakes, the parents listened with delight to Ivashka's account of all that had happened to him. After that they continued to live together in happiness.

The Eighth Skazka

THE HEADLESS PRINCESS

Alexei Fyodorovitch lived in a tiny kingdom that borders greater Russia. Within that kingdom, Alexei lived in the small capital city, where his father was a priest. Also within that city was the king's palace, which was little more than a large stone building with walls that pressed against the main street. Each day, young Alexei walked past the palace on his way to visit the elderly lady who was his tutor. It would have been better for Alexei if he had walked by a different street.

One winter eve, as darkness descended early on the city streets, Alexei was returning from his lessons. He walked rapidly, with the icy air finding every tiny opening of his hand-me-down coat. His young body was too cold to allow him to mosey along the darkened street, as was his habit. Still, when he walked past a lighted window of the palace, he naturally shot a glance into the illumined interior. At once he stopped walking. His eyes caught sight of a most unusual activity within. Alexei became so engrossed in what he was watching that he momentarily forgot the chill blasts that had tormented him throughout his walk to home. Within the palace he could see the king's daughter, primping. He stood, transfixed, while the princess lifted her head from her shoulders, carefully combed the long, dark strands and then replaced her head on her shoulders. He muttered to himself, "What a marvel that was! Why, she's a downright witch!"

46

Having said that, Alexei suddenly felt frightened. He immediately turned and walked rapidly along the street. He glanced behind; but there was only the empty street behind him. Even so, he decided to run the remaining distance to his home.

The following day, he described what he had seen to several children whom he met on the street. All the children—even the bigger boys—shuddered as he related his experience to them. But he said nothing to his family or to his teacher.

Several days passed. The princess became ill. Her malady worsened. She summoned her father and told him that if she died, he should have the priest's son read the book of psalms over her coffin for three nights running! That very night the princess died and her body was placed in a handsome wooden casket and placed in the church. In the morning, the king summoned the priest.

"Do you have a son?"

"Yes, your majesty," answered the priest. "He's a fine young man, who respects his elders and tends to his studies..."

"Well," said the king, "beginning tonight, I want him to read the psalter over my daughter's coffin for three nights running."

The priest rushed home to relay the royal request, proud that his son had been chosen for this modest service to their grieving monarch.

Alexei heard the request in silence, before walking to the home of his elderly tutor. As he began his lesson, the old woman sensed his apprehension. She asked him what troubled him.

"Speak plainly child."

"Oh Granny, I'm lost! I must read the psalter over the coffin of the princess for three nights running... and, do you know, she's a witch?"

"Oh, yes, Aloysha, my child. I've known that for a very long time."

47

The kindly, old teacher, wizened by the decades, watched as tears welled in the lad's eyes before spilling over to create salty streaks down the youthful cheeks. Then, she spoke sharply.

"Now, now, Aloysha. Stop crying this instant!"

Then her voice softened.

"Tears have never drowned danger. Listen to my words and think clearly. I can help you."

As Alexei raised his head, he saw the woman move to a nearby sideboard. There, beside her samovar, she studied several dining utensils before clutching an old knife. She returned to hand the knife to the priest's son. As he accepted it, he observed that the blade was neither sharp nor pointed.

"What's this, Granny?"

"This," replied the old one, is a simple knife; but it will—if you keep your wits about you—protect you from any witch's deviltry!"

Moving a bony finger in a circular motion through the air, in order to illustrate her advice, she observed:

"Each night, before you sit to read the psalter, use this knife to draw a circle around you.

Then read your sacred verses in a clear and strong voice—as the prophets of old must have done. Then, no matter what the princess does to frighten you, never, never step beyond that circle! If you do, she will have you... and you'll perish!"

That evening, as the twilit sky was streaked with a fiery red glow, one of the king's attendants led Alexei to the church. The attendant then lit the huge candle that sat upon a heavy oaken stand, and turned to walk from the church.

As quickly as he saw the attendant step through the door and close it behind himself, Alexei drew the circle on the floor, encompassing little more than his chair and the candle stand. Then he seated himself, opened the book of psalms and began to read.

Despite the urge to whisper the words in order not to disturb the corpse of the princess, Alexei read loudly, with a trembling voice. By the time he reached the opening chapter's fourth verse, he was becoming more relaxed and his voice had lost its tremble.

"The ungodly are not so, but are like the chaff which the wind driveth away..."

With a very loud creaking sound, the coffin lid flew open. The princess sat upright and looked directly into the eyes of the shocked youth. She screamed at him.

"Chaff which the wind driveth away! You vicious little sneak, peaking into someone's windows and telling people what you see! I'll show you what the wind drives away! I'll show you how quickly you become chaff and we'll let the wind drive you right down into the mouth of a flaming volcano!"

Alexei nearly fell from his chair! He gasped for air as the evening calm was suddenly broken by the sound of fierce winds outside. He determined to read and ignore the loud whistling sounds of a terrible windstorm. He read resolutely although he couldn't hear his own voice above the wailing sounds from outside the church. The building seemed to tremble and Alexei imagined the entire structure crumbling with him lost beneath the rubble. Still, he kept reading.

He cowered as the winds roared through the open church windows and he heard sounds like shattering glass. Although he kept reading, he heard objects being tossed about the church. But, he continued to read.

As he read, Alexei sensed the princess nearby. He could see that she was ranting and charging toward him, only to stop at the edge of the circle.

Then, all became still so that he would breathe a sigh of relief; a sigh that was quickly interrupted by another blast of wind that was fiercer and louder than the last. Now he became more terrified, almost ready to jump from his chair and run. However, he suddenly realized that the tremendous winds that were racing through the church might extinguish his candle, leaving him in total darkness with the fiendish princess somewhere in the blackness, waiting to pounce on him.

He shot a glance at the candle. The flame was steady. It wasn't even flickering. Momentarily, he was perplexed. How soon would the winds catch that single flame? It suddenly occurred to him: the candle was unaffected by the devilish hurricane because it sat, securely, within Alexei's circle. This meant that he, too, was secure, just at his old tutor had promised. Reassured by this thought, he returned to his reading.

Hours later, he saw movement nearby and glanced up. The princess was climbing back into the coffin, adjusting her robe and gently lowering the massive lid. Within a few moments, the church was bathed in the warm tones of the morning sunlight.

Later that day, after Alexei had a long rest, he hurried to his teacher. She assured him that he had acted bravely and properly; but she also warned him to be even more resolute in his actions; because the coming night would surely be more terrifying than the first. It was.

He began his reading for the second night with the opening verses once again. As Alexei read the fourth verse, he steeled himself for the same shrieking attack she had used on the previous night. Instead, she gently opened the coffin lid, quietly stepped from the box and stood beside the coffin, staring at the crucifix as though she had no concern or awareness of Alexei and his firm reading of the psalter.

He eventually finished more than twenty psalms; but kept reading.

"Yea, though I walk through the valley of the shadow of death, I will fear no evil..."

That verse seemed to agitate her to the point of again cursing Alexei as viciously and loudly as before.

"Picture that dark vale, you wretch! You will be entering it within a few moments and you'll welcome it as an escape from here. I've invited some guests to come and escort you into the valley of death!"

She began muttering strange names, slowly and deliberately. Each name she spoke brought forth a ghoulish beast. Creatures, far more ghastly and ugly than anything poor Alexei could have imagined were appearing suddenly around him! Several popped up from behind the pews. A pair of fiendish forms appeared from behind the altar. Another, of terrifying features, dropped from the massive rafters to stand beside the princess. Then all the creatures slowly edged closer to Alexei and closer to the circle! Could they break through? Would they break through?

Some brandished swords and pitchforks. Others had lighted torches. Then all charged at the circle, with the terrified Alexei barely able to think. Yet, when none broke into the circle, Alexei mustered the strength to continue reading. Hours later, they suddenly vanished. Within a few moments the princess shouted a vow to return to crush the priest's son. Once she was within the coffin, she pulled shut the lid so that the church looked as serene and inspiring as ever.

Again, with a stern warning from his tutor, Alexei returned for the third and last night of duty as servant to the king and psalm reader for the unsuspecting king's wicked daughter. He was barely seated when the princess hastily exited her coffin and began shouting threats and curses at him. The worst horrors of the previous two nights were combined into one, continuous terror.

An intense thunderstorm swirled around the church, with every thunderclap rattling through the building. Dozens of bolts of lightning flashed within the church, with smoke everywhere. Alexei, still nervously reading, saw tiny flames racing along the bottoms of the walls. Then the flames began climbing the walls, crackling and snapping before roaring into an inferno of light! Alexei whimpered and shook with fright; but held fast.

Suddenly he heard a deafening sound which he easily identified with an earthquake. A gaping crack opened in the church floor, and pews toppled into the crevice to disappear. The altar wobbled briefly and then crumbled and plunged into the opening and out of sight! More terrified than ever, Alexei repeated one of his earlier verses as a means of begging for deliverance:

"Hear me speedily, O Lord; my spirit faileth. Hide not thy face from me, lest I be like unto them that go down into the pit. Cause me to hear thy loving kindness in the morning, for in Thee do I trust."

He barely finished reading his suppliant verse when he heard a familiar voice calling from outside the room.

"Aloysha! Aloysha! Let me in. I'll save you! Hurry! Let me in!"

It was the voice of his kindly old tutor!

His eyes brightened. His tutor was just beyond the door. She could protect him. If he could just dash to the door, outrunning the fiendish princess, this horror would end!

He glanced to the distant corner, looking directly at the fiendish smile of the princess. At that very instant, he again heard his teacher's summons:

"Aloysha, let me in quickly. I'll take you home without harm."

However, Alexey noticed the princess' mouth moving silently. He was sure that the wicked woman's lips had mouthed the last words he'd heard, "you home without harm." He shuddered violently with the realization that he'd almost made a fatal mistake; but his resolve returned.

He closed his eyes and sat motionless. Seconds ticked away with no sound, no stirring. What was his tormentor doing. Finally he jerked in terror when she shrieked loudly, "You wretched little boy! Your craftiness won't save you for long. We're not finished here... there are more horrors afoot!"

Alexei suddenly remembered his primary duty here. He opened his eyes, stared directly at the pages of the psalter still clutched in his hands, and began reading aloud. At that moment, he heard a great crackling sound. Glancing up, he saw that every wall was engulfed in flames, with small fires spouting from the floor in every direction. Alexei whimpered with fright, but read on, surrounded by flame. Yet, within his circle he felt no heat. Just terror...

Still, he heard the sounds of the roaring fire. Still, he heard the shrill, shrieking threats of the demon princess. Still, he focused on his psalter and its inspiring words.

All at once, there was a deafening, cracking sound. Alexei instantly thought of the day that he and his father had watched lumbermen felling giant trees in the nearby forest. As the trees weakened, they cracked very loudly for several moments before one eardrum-shattering crack as they snapped and plunged to the earth! As Alexei recalled this, he remembered that, although he had watched the lumbermen from a safe location, the great cracking sound still frightened him!

Now, that same sound caused him added fear as he sat by the witch's coffin. In his mind Alexei saw those massive wooden beams, beneath the church's roof, beginning to creak and snap. Soon, he realized, they might come crashing down on him! Although he struggled to overcome his fear, his doubts grew enormously. There was a circle of protection around him; but was he protected from overhead? Would his loving parents find only his puny body, crushed beneath the giant timbers?

The cracking of timber grew louder and Alexei began sobbing until he could scarcely breathe. Afraid to look up, he determined to meet his doom with a few more words of scripture on his tongue; the last small verse from his book of *Psalms*.

"Let everything that hath breath praise the Lord. Praise ye the Lord."

Then he sensed that something strange was occurring; but he was too terrified to grasp its meaning.

Silence.

That's what Alexei sensed. Aside from his weakened, stumbling voice, there was no other sound.

He slowly raised his head to look around the church. There were no flames... no cracking timbers. He looked to the corner occupied by the princess. She was motionless, glaring at him. What was her next evil trick?

His eyes swept around the interior of the church. Where will her next terror appear? Then he caught sight of something. It was a small panel of light shining on the church's west wall.

The fiend shouted: "Curse you!... Curse you! Curse you!"

Was this another spell, conjured to again deceive him into some unguarded foolishness?

Not this time.

The princess shrieked: "No! No! No! No!," her voice trailing with each word.

As Alexei watched the panel of light move lower on the wall, the princess tore at her clothing in utter desperation and then flung herself, face down, into the gaping coffin!

Now Alexei began sobbing softly, with relief. He was too shaken to move; but was still tightly gripping his father's psalter.

As he sat there, the church door opened and the king and two attendants entered. The king saw no evidence of the night's horrors, for the church appeared to be quite normal except for the disarray of the coffin and its contents.

"What's the meaning of this?" he demanded, upon seeing the disheveled corpse of his daughter.

Alexei showed the king the knife given to him by his tutor. Then he explained all that had occurred. The king listened attentively, all the while shaking his head in sorrow while tears streaked down his face. When Alexei finished his harrowing narration, the king ordered his attendants to drive an ashen stake through the daughter's heart and to proceed with her burial. Shortly thereafter, the king appointed Alexei's father to the position of bishop as reward for raising such a brave and dutiful son.

The Ninth Skazka

LUKAN'S LADDER

[A moujik (moo JEEK) is a peasant. A verst is an old Russian measure equal to about two-thirds of a mile.]

Lukan Andreyevich (Luke, son of Andrey) was a poor, old moujik. He lived with his wife, Lubava, who was equally poor and similarly old. They lived in a shabby cottage a few versts from the old fortress town of Novgorod (New Fort).

One day, Lukan heard the rooster crowing loudly. Seeking the source of the sound, he found the rooster in the space below the floor boards. The cackling bird seemed to be announcing the discovery of a pea lying in the dirt beneath the floor. Lukan quickly shooed the bird and poured water on the solitary pea.

The very next morning, he and Lubava noticed that the pea had sprouted and was already poking through a tiny crack between the boards. Reasoning that such a healthy sprout should produce a bountiful stalk of peas, Lukan tore loose the floor's planking in that area.

Each day the impoverished old couple watched in astonishment as the plant, drawing miraculous strength from the black earth beneath their hovel, climbed skyward. In fact, within a week's time they lost sight of the top of the stalk, which had obviously reached into heaven. Curious as to what became of the upper reaches of their colossal pea stalk, Lukan made a proposal.

"Wife, wife. I say, I want to climb this plant and see what's at the top. Maybe I'll find us some sugar there, or mead, perhaps... lots of nice things!"

Lubava, equally curious and excited, declared, "Yes, Lukan, climb away if you've a mind to. I'll heat the samovar so that we can enjoy a cup of tea when you return."

Promising his wife to quickly return with whatever he might find, Lukan began to climb. As he climbed and climbed, he was reassured by the incredible strength of the stalk and its branches. At last, still as curious as ever, he reached an opening in the clouds and peered at the heavenly landscape. His surroundings appeared similar to his own neighborhood, except that the only structure in sight was a beautiful cottage.

The cottage door was ajar, so Lukan stepped inside. The scene within was fully illuminated by heavenly light shining through windows larger than any the poor peasant could have imagined.

At the same time, his nostrils were almost overwhelmed by the savory scents of the freshly-cooked food that sat on top of a massive stove at the far end of the room. The steaming pots held geese, pigs, puddings and pastries. And poor Lukan, near starving from the long climb, would have begun feasting except for one thing: the goat with seven eyes!

The seven-eyed goat guarded its absent master's stove. The hungering moujik was not only very hungry; he was weary to the marrow of his bones. Still, he was determined to outlast the alert goat. He talked and talked to the goat. In a voice that was both soothing and friendly, he charmed the goat into falling asleep, one eye at a time. As last, six eyes closed in sleep. Unnoticed by Lukan, the faithful goat kept one eye open. With that lone eye, the goat watched Lukan cram his body with great quantities of the most succulent and flavorful foods. All was washed lower into his gut with large glasses of wine. The split-hoofed beast watched Lukan pause in his eating just once; and only long enough to insert a small canister of sugar into the depths of one of his pockets. Finally, made even more tired by consuming such a glut of tasty foods, Lukan belched several times and then laid his head on the thick wooden tabletop and allowed his own two eyes to close.

When the cottager finally arrived home, Lukan awakened with a start, only to hear the goat telling its master of all that was eaten and drunk by Lukan. The cottager flew into a rage. He called to his servants, who came running into the cottage. They lifted Lukan, the overstuffed moocher, from his chair and tossed him from the cottage!

Lukan painfully arose from the ground and hurriedly returned to the opening through which he had earlier climbed into heaven. There was no pea stalk to be seen. He cautiously peeked down through the opening, only to reel in fright from the sight of pure emptiness between himself and his home so far below. However, at that moment a spider's web floated by and caught itself on his face and beard, clinging there.

Lukan, annoyed by the web, pulled the cobweb free from his face. Suddenly reminded of the unique strength of spider webs, he began gathering cobwebs until he had a large bundle. With these he fashioned a substantial cord. He next tethered one end of the cobweb rope to a heavenly tree and proceeded to descend. Farther and farther he lowered himself, until he came to the lower end of his cord. Glancing below, he saw that the earth was still far beneath. Without hesitation he crossed himself, closed his eyes and loosened his grip on the braided cobwebs...

At the end of a long drop, Lukan splashed into a swamp, his feet and legs driven deep into the muck by the impact. Having little remaining strength and no leverage, he remained mired and immobile. Shortly, a large duck flew across the swamp. It circled three times and then landed on Lukan's head. He remained still while the duck built a nest on his head. Finally, it laid an egg in the nest. As it stretched, ready to fly away and look for food, Lukan grabbed its tail feathers and clung to them with his last remaining strength. As the duck flapped its wings wildly, and slowly lifted its body into the air, it also pulled Lukan free from his swampy trap.

With the live duck clutched in one arm and the duck egg deep in another pocket, Lukan hurried home to his dilapidated cottage, where Lubava told him of her fear for his safety when the pea stalk had suddenly collapsed into a heap. As he assured her that he was unhurt, Lukan presented his cackling duck and its egg to Lubava. Then, while they sipped their hot – and well-sweetened tea – he told her of his wild adventure. Then the two of them patched their floor, ceiling and roof. The couple then took all their baskets and gathered enough peas to supply them through the coming winter.

The Tenth Skazka

THE STEED AND THE STONE

Late one evening, Boris the farrier was walking home from visiting a nearby village. As he neared his hometown, he saw his long-time friend, Vassili walking toward him. His mind somewhat addled by alcohol, Boris totally forgot that Vassili had died several years earlier.

"Good health, Boris. Good health," said the corpse.

"And to you, good health."

Then the ghost of Vassili invited Boris to visit his house.

"Come along to my cottage. We'll drink a cup or two for old time's sake."

Boris, who loved alcohol and friendship equally, accepted the invitation and followed to Vassili's house. There they spent several quickly-passing hours happily chatting and chuckling.

"Well, now. It's time for me to go home," said the farrier, as he stood unsteadily.

"Comrade, stay the night. Why do you want to leave now? You have no lamp... and it's too dark a night for walking."

Boris could only reply, "No. No. I'm too busy. Tomorrow will be here before I've slept enough... and I have work that must be done tomorrow. Thank you."

"Well, goodbye... but, why must you walk? Borrow my horse. He can follow the road to town on the darkest of nights. Just return it to me tomorrow."

Boris dizzily mounted the horse; but, before he'd even got a steady hold of the reins, the steed was in motion! The speed was incredible! Boris let go the reins and gripped around the horse's neck to keep from falling. Still, the horse plunged on, through the night. His intoxicated rider couldn't think clearly; but he did notice that there was no sound from the hoof beats. It was as though the hoofs never touched the dirt beneath.

Just as suddenly as the horse had begun the ride, it came to an end! The horse stood perfectly still. Boris was far too frightened to move. He still held fast to the steed's neck, his eyes shut tightly. Minutes passed, with all unchanged, until the crowing of a rooster caused Boris to open his eyes slowly. He was stunned by what he saw.

He was in the middle of a graveyard, surrounded by tombstones. Not only that; but, he was clinging to one of the stones, just as he might cling to a wild horse... while another stone had formed his saddle for the ride home. Shaking with fright, Boris 'dismounted' from the tombstone and nervously walked to the edge of the graveyard. Then he started walking home with a very brisk gait and he never looked back.

The Eleventh Skazka

THE FIDDLER IN HELL

Filipp [fee LEEP] was a wandering fiddler who traveled the countryside playing his fiddle for the few kopecks that would be contributed by grateful listeners. He particularly liked to attend weddings and other festive celebrations, since his contributions at these events were more substantial.

Thus it happened that one day, he found himself walking toward a wedding at a village near the headwaters of the Pechora River in the foothills of the Urals. He had only idle thoughts and few cares in the world, when the earth suddenly collapsed beneath his feet! Down he dropped, fiddle and bow in hand, into hell. Not only did he land in hell; but he tumbled from an upper level right into its very depths, to the level reserved for the most wicked individuals. As luck would have it, he landed in the exact area as that occupied by Konstantin, the once-wealthy moujik.

"Well... hello, friend. I'm Filipp, a poor fiddler; but I'm only here in hell because the earth crumbled under my weight, near the little village above!"

Konstantin stared at the new arrival, then replied.

"Hail to you, comrade. I believe that I know you. I heard you fiddling at several events. Your fiddling skill made me laugh and cry. And did you not give a very sweet rendering of some gypsy songs at a recent event?"

"Why, yes," declared Filipp. "A widow requested the tunes for a funeral in the very village under which we are meeting. I'd never before been asked to play those particular..."

The fiddler suddenly stopped talking, briefly silenced by a powerful thought. Then he blurted, "Oh! Dear me! Could I have been fiddling those songs at your funeral!"

"So it was, Filya. So it was. However, I was unable to thank you from within my walnut casket."

After a moment, Konstantin continued.

"I must tell you, comrade. It's an ill wind that brought you here. We're in hell, you know, and the fiends who dwell here will soon return."

"Well, friend," inquired Filipp, "just who are you and why are you here in hell?"

"I'm Konstantin," replied the condemned man. "I was just a peasant, a moujik, from the above village. Still, I was able to gain a fair amount of wealth. The problem is, I kept every coin for myself."

He continued, "I was so afraid of losing even a kopeck, that I hid my fortune. I buried it at two locations. I had planned to tell my three grown sons about the money when I got older; but, sad to say, I never got older. I died much earlier than I expected to die."

"Well, that's a truly sad story," offered Filipp.

"Oh, that's not the half of it, fiddler," the man sobbed. "Since I never gave even a single coin to the poor, I'm being punished here in hell. The fiends are regularly whipping me with briars and thorns. In fact, those terrible fiends who live here in the underworld are up on earth at this very moment, collecting more nettles for whipping me and tearing at my flesh!"

"Whatever am I to do," cried Filipp the Fiddler, looking nervously about himself. "They may take to whipping me, too."

Konstantin listened to the fiddler's words. He thought about them briefly as he looked toward the underworld gate through which the fiends of hell would soon be returning.

"Perhaps I can help you. Listen to me, Filya... go and sit on that stove. Hide behind the pipe and eat nothing for three years. Then you'll be safe."

Filipp rushed to hide behind the stovepipe. He was hardly hidden when the fiends' loud gibberish announced their return. They proceeded to whip and lash poor Konstantin, sarcastically damning him all the while, as follows:

"This is for you, rich man. Here's your reward for your false thrift. You buried your money; but you couldn't hide it from us, even if we can't gather it. The hiding place beneath the gate is far too busy for us to get the money without being trampled by the horses above. And it's much too risky to try reaching up to grab your money hidden beneath the corn-kiln, as we may be flailed by your sons or their workers as they thresh the corn. So, moujik, as they flail your corn, so we'll flail your miserable flesh!"

As quickly as the vicious fiends left, Konstantin called to the frightened fiddler.

"Please, I beg of you... if you get out of here, go to my sons and tell them to unearth the money I've hidden and to give it to the poor. Maybe you can save me from this everlasting agony. Tell them that one fortune is hidden beneath the farmyard gate and the other is buried under the corn-kiln. If they could only give that money to the poor..."

As Filipp was promising to help, if he was fortunate enough to escape from hell, the fiends returned, in numbers even greater than before.

64

Filipp was able to again hide behind the stovepipe. However, he froze in terror when he heard the harsh voice of one fiend speaking to Konstantin.

"Well, moujik, what have you got here that smells so Russian?"

The quick-thinking Konstantin remarked, "That's an easy question to answer. You have been in Russia and you brought away the Russian smell with you."

"How could that be?" they answered, as they began looking for the cowering fiddler. They soon located the intruder.

"Aha! Here's a fiddler," one fiend announced loudly.

The fiends pulled Filipp from behind the chimney and made him entertain them with playing the fiddle. In fact, he played for them for three years, although he thought that it was a mere three days. Finally, he tired and said,

"Here's the wonder. I used to play for just one single evening and my fiddle strings would snap. But, now, although I've been playing for three entire days, the strings are intact. Bless me! Bless me!"

No sooner had he uttered those words, than all his strings snapped.

"There now, brothers," complained the fiddler, "you can see for yourselves. I can no longer play."

"Wait a bit," offered one of the fiends, "I've got two hanks of catgut. I'll get them for you."

The fiend ran away; but within a few moments he was back and carrying strings of catgut. The fiddler, who had hoped to escape, dejectedly attached the strings to his fiddle. He again spoke, "May the Lord grant us his blessings."

Again, the strings snapped. Again, Filipp was unable to play.

"No, brothers; your catgut simply didn't suit the fiddle. You tried your best: but I must still have some of my own from home. With your permission, I'll go home for new strings."

"No, no, fiddler. If we let you leave, you'll never return."

Filipp frowned. "Well, if you don't trust me, send one of your own to escort me."

The fiends selected one of their own and sent him to accompany Filipp. Soon the fiddler and his keeper were back in the village. There he could hear that, in the farthest cottage, a wedding was being celebrated.

"Let's go to the wedding," the fiddler shouted.

"I love festivities," agreed the fiend. "So come along!"

They soon walked into the cottage, where many guests recognized the locally-celebrated fiddler. They called to him.

"Filipp, where have you been hiding so long. It's been three years!"

"I have been in the other world," he responded calmly.

The fiddler and the fiend sat there and enjoyed themselves for some time. Finally, the fiend snapped, "Come, fiddler, it's time we were on our way."

"But, wait a bit longer," moaned Filipp. "I need to fiddle for a while to cheer the young people, here."

Thus, they remained seated until the roosters crowed to announce the new day. When the fiddler glanced at his underworld companion, he saw that the fiend had disappeared, having scurried back to hell.

Filipp quickly located Constantin's sons and pulled them aside.

"Your father bids you to unearth his money—there's a potful buried at the gate and another buried beneath the corn-kiln. Give every kopeck to the poor, to remove your father's terrible punishment."

The sons agreed to work together to gather the money. Once unearthed, they began handing coins to the poor. However, the more than distributed, the more they seemed to have. The faster they worked, the more the money grew. So they walked along the roadway until they came to the main crossroads in the area; one that connected two villages and two larger towns. At the crossroads, the three sons asked every passer-by to take as much money as he or she could grip in one hand. Still, a fortune remained in the pots.

Their next plan for unloading the cursed coins was to petition the tsar to promote a major building project and use Konstantin's money to finance the work. This the tsar willingly did. He signed an order for a bridge to be built at an old town near the capital city. The town stood on the banks of a swift river, within sight of the capital; but, the people had to travel more than fifty versts in order to get to an upriver bridge that allowed them to cross over and reach their capital city.

With the tsar's support, a bridge was ordered to be built; a bridge that would cut the villagers' travel distance to about five versts. At last, the bridge was completed and, when all the workers and contractors were paid, the pots were finally empty and many people marveled at the benefit they would enjoy. Shortly after the bridge was opened, a young boy happened to stroll across the bridge in order to visit the river's opposite shore. The child, in all his youthful innocence, praised the handsome arch, saying, "God bless the person who gave us this fine bridge."

When the Lord heard the prayer of the innocent child, he ordered his angels to release Konstantin, the once-rich moujik, from the depths of hell.

The Twelfth Skazka

SOZH AND DNIEPER

[The following skazka tells of the legendary origins of two of Russia's streams, the rivers Sozh and Dnieper. They are described as being the sons of yet another river, the Dvina. The sources of all three lie in the region west of old Moskva (Moscow). The Dvina is identified in this skazka as being the father of the other two. The Dvina River follows a northwesterly course to its mouth on the Gulf of Riga, while the other two—Dvina's sons—flow south, as the tale reveals.]

Very long ago—even beyond the memory of our grandparents—the rivers were living people. One such was Dvina, a blind, Russian liveryman. He and his wife were the aging parents of two grown sons, Sozh and Dnieper. Despite his lost eyesight, Dvina still managed to help Dnieper run the stable and, although his earnings were less than in his younger years, Dvina had saved enough money to live his remaining years in modest comfort.

Sadly, each parent had a favorite child. Dvina had always favored the elder son, Sozh, while his wife favored the younger. Sozh was fond of rambling and would be gone for days on end, roaming through the hills, forests and plains. He was utterly unconcerned about anyone else and had no interest in working or saving money. Dvina had tried, without success, to instruct Sozh in the importance of conserving his funds. Dvina's constant theme: Money wasted is money stolen from someone in need. Yet, despite all his faults, Dvina favored his elder, spendthrift son.

The younger son, Dnieper, on the other hand, stayed close to home and joyfully sacrificed to help his family. He never asked for special favor and spent little money on his own interests. It was he whom their mother favored.

This was the situation when Dnieper was old enough to lament to his mother that he wished to strike out on his own. Further, he didn't wish to wait his turn, since Sozh showed no signs of ever becoming independent of his parents. So his mother conspired to help him. When she had fully developed her plans, she gave her husband, Dvina, enough liquor to cause intoxication. Then she told her besotted husband that his favored, elder son, Sozh, was arriving. As she ushered in Dnieper, her favorite, she told her sightless mate that it was Sozh, awaiting his father's blessing. Dvina, ever trustful, proceeded to bless Dnieper, thusly:

"My son, I'm pleased to give you my blessing. It is one that will give you a lasting and productive life. You will dissolve into a great river; one that is wide and deep. You will forever flow past villages and towns. Your waters will wash the shores and carry the goods for people

throughout all of your long journey from our northern home to the dark sea far to the south. Your brother will be your servant, bringing you extra waters to swell your flow as you approach the great sea."

Dnieper, the benefactor of this deception, changed into a river and began to fulfill the blessing, cutting a crooked, watery channel southward.

However, three days later, Sozh returned home. He was angry upon learning that he had been denied the full blessing of his father. As he fumed to his father, Dvina gave him this advice: Sozh was to move swiftly and secretly and try to retrieve the privilege given to Dnieper.

"Hold your temper, my angry son. You, Sozh, will also gain my blessing. But, for you to become the dominant river of the two, you will have to push south through gullies and swamps and other hidden places. Remain hidden until you've overtaken Dnieper, then rush into his path, forcing him to become your tributary! In that way, he will always be your servant."

Sozh rejoiced at the prospect of becoming the region's greatest river. Promptly transformed, he raced southward, pushing through hidden places and creating new gullies and gathering small streams. As he secretly splashed through unseen marshes and ravines, a vulture spied him and flew west to tell Dnieper that he was being pursued. So Dnieper created his channel even faster.

Then Sozh asked a raven's help. "Now, Mr. Raven, I'm going to create my channel underground to remain unseen. Meanwhile, you fly ahead of Dnieper. Then, Mr. Raven, when you are clearly at a location just ahead of Dnieper, croak three times. I will know where to pop out of the ground and capture Dnieper into my waters!"

Sozh burrowed underground and moved, unseen, parallel to the path of his younger sibling. However, high above the Russian countryside, the vulture attacked the raven, causing the raven to caw from the attack! When Sozh heard the raven's croaking, he suddenly burst from the earth, only to find himself rushing headlong into the waters of Dnieper! The race was ended.

To this very day, one can see – about 100 miles north of the historic old city of Kiev, the joining of the two streams at the town of Loyev. At that town, Sozh, the shorter, riverine brother, meekly empties his waters into the waves of the great river, Dnieper, which rushes southward for another 600 miles before pouring into the Black Sea.

The Thirteenth Skazka

THE SHROUD

In some villages it came to be expected that lazy girls would host parties, with tasty sweets and tea in order to have the guests help with some of the tiresome work of the hostess. Veronika (or "Nika") was one such lazybones. When she had more spinning than she cared to do, she'd host a spinning party for the other young girls of her neighborhood.

The last such party that "Nika" hosted occurred one warm Spring evening. When the guests arrived, they found that Veronika had a large supply of sweetmeats, such as candied fruits and nuts, candy sticks, sugared cakes and similar treats. They obviously enjoyed doing Nika's spinning, while nibbling on the assorted sweetmeats.

While they worked they gossiped and chatted at a pace that would shame an orator. The sorry thing was that the conversation eventually came to the subject of which girl present was the boldest of the lot. Finally, the lazybones pronounced, "I'm not afraid of anything!"

One of her guests challenged her.

"That's not true, Nika. You're as scared as any of us."

"I am not!"

Another girl, added her opinion.

"Nika. You know it's true. Why just today my mother said, 'That Veronika is afraid of work.'"

Veronika was stung by the remark.

"You know that that's not what I'm talking about! I'm saying that I'm bolder than anyone here."

"Then prove it," another challenged.

"Well... how? You say it and I'll do it."

A different girl, silent on the subject until now, chimed, "I know how to prove it. If you're really not afraid, go past the graveyard to the church and grab the icon from the door and bring it for us to see!"

"Yes, do that, Nika," they all agreed. "Do that and we'll agree that you are the boldest."

Such a challenge was doubly exciting for the girls to contemplate. Not only did it involve walking past a churchyard full of tombs in the darkness; but, it meant committing a sacrilege, since the icons were paintings of famous holy figures and the icons themselves were considered by all to be about as sacred as the saints themselves. Just the thought of someone stealing one sent a shiver through many of the girls.

"If that's what it takes to quiet you girls, I'll do it. However, each of you must spin a distaff of flax for me."

The guests all realized that each would now be expected to take the cleft or split wooden staff and to wind flax or woolen fibers onto it in order to form a continuous woolen thread. They set to work at fulfilling their part of the pact, while looking askance at their hostess to see whether or not she seemed frightened. If Veronika was frightened by the prospect before her, no one could detect it. She calmly walked from the cottage as her parents stood by the fireplace, shaking their heads in despair.

When Veronika returned, she was carrying the picture. She showed it to all and offered it to one after another of the girls to examine. All shrank from the nearness of the pilfered icon. She than declared, "Alright. I brought the picture. Who is going to return it to the church?"

All the guests were silent, looking at the floor or the fire or looking anyplace but in Veronika's direction.

"I should have known. You are all so bold in poking fun at me; but you're afraid to walk to the church alone... Alright, I'll return it myself. As I told you, 'I am not afraid.'"

Veronika walked past the graveyard and up to the church door, where she rehung the holy image. Then, as she returned home, she saw—in the graveyard—a corpse sitting atop a tombstone.

The corpse was wrapped in a long, white shroud. She boldly walked to the corpse and pulled away the shroud. The corpse stared at Veronika without speaking. She carried the shroud in a bundle and hurried home, where she announced her latest theft.

"I took the picture back to the church where I had got it. On the way home I stopped in the graveyard and grabbed this shroud from a corpse."

All the girls were horrified; but some told the others that Nika just had to be teasing. That was the situation when they moved to the table to sup. Then they laid down to sleep.

It was almost dawn when all, including Veronika's unlucky parents, were wide awake and listening to the loud rapping sound on a window. They could see that it was a corpse, staring coldly at them. Although the others may not have noticed, even Veronika was trembling!

"Give me my shroud. Give me my shroud... or I'll come in there and get it myself!"

While the others continued to shake, without control, Nika opened the window and handed the shroud to the corpse, who shocked all by declining.

"I'll not take it. You are the one who stole it, so put it back where you got it!"

No one spoke. Everyone involved looked as though they belonged in a stage set. The tension and silence lingered for several seconds, before a rooster's crow sent the corpse racing back to the graveyard, leaving Veronika still holding the corpse's shroud. The spinners quickly excused themselves and promptly hurried home.

The next night, exactly twenty-four hours from his last visit, the corpse again peeked into the window. Veronika, her parents and siblings, could see that it was, surely enough, the corpse, his features even more grotesque than they had recalled them. Again, he tapped on the window. Again, he demanded his shroud.

Veronika's parents quickly grabbed the shroud, opened the window and pushed the shroud into his arms. This still wasn't acceptable.

"No, no. You didn't take the shroud and you cannot return it. Only Veronika can properly return it... and return it to the exact place where she stole it!"

Again, the delay caused the sunrise and the rooster's crow. The corpse quickly left the scene. Now the desperate parents decided to contact the priest. They visited him and asked what might be done.

"Couldn't a special sermon be conducted to try to rid the valley of this creature?"

After some thought, the priest instructed them to have Veronika attend the next day's early service. They promised.

The next morning, the lazybones went to church. The service was well attended by people from this village. All were eager to see how their priest might handle the dilemma.

Just as they were about to sing the cherubim song, a whirlwind ripped through the church. It knocked all the people of the congregation flat on their faces. Despite the many worshippers in attendance, the whirlwind actually picked up just one, Veronika! It slammed her to the ground so forcefully that she simply disappeared into Mother Earth. Just as suddenly as it appeared, the whirlwind disappeared; but, as the astonished parishioners stared at the site of her disappearance, they saw nothing of her mortal remains, but one item: the rope of black hair that had once been Veronika's long and lovely braid.

The Fourteenth Skazka

THE WARRIOR AND THE WARLOCK

Timofey Pavlovitch Kalganov was a soldier who had served at a distant Eastern post for all of his three years in the service of the Tsar. From the day of his induction, he longed to return to his family. Although he had trained and become a skilled warrior, who was promoted to the rank of corporal, he still longed to visit his native village. When he finally applied for a furlough, it was easily granted and he bought a fine riding horse and started for home. While he was still a couple of versts from home, he arrived at the home of the miller, Zaretski.

During his late childhood, Timofey had carried many a bag of grain for Zaretski , who always treated the teenager with respect and kindness. The two became close friends, with Zaretski being nearly as sad with Timofey's departure for the army as Timofey's own family members. Now the two sat and reminisced for several hours. When the miller mentioned the recent death of his only horse—the one that pulled his grain-filled cart, Timofey offered him the use of the riding horse that had brought him safely across the Siberian wilds.

"But how," queried old Zaretski, "would you return to your post?"

Timofey shrugged his shoulders lightly.

"I shall simply buy another."

Then he continued, "You know, old man, how miserly I was as a youth. Well, that hasn't left me. Add to that my isolation in a far-flung military camp, where there was little to buy, and you must know that I've saved a few roubles."

As he spoke, he lay open his jacket to reveal a leather pouch with tightly drawn strings. He was clearly proud of the weighty bag of coins that he'd accumulated through thrift.

The miller, utterly lost without a draft animal, was more than willing to accept the horse, even if it was only a riding horse. Timofey was more than willing to help. It was the nature of Timofey, to step in where help was needed, and always with the sure confidence of one who feels that he is properly trained to assist as needed.

Suddenly, Timofey realized that the night was descending about the pair of comrades. The air was chilling his bare arms.

"I must leave now. It's already dusk and I don't wish to be walking to my village in darkness."

"No! No! Stay," urged Zaretsky. "Spend the night here. You'll have the extra blanket and you will be much safer if you walk home during the day. You can breakfast with me and be on the road by daybreak. It's downright frightening out there, tonight!"

"Come now, Comrade Miller, what can make me fearful?"

With no response from the miller, Timofey pressed harder.

"Well?"

"Listen to me, Timofey Pavlovitch. I think that God is punishing us. Just last year, shortly after the feast of Pentecost, a warlock died here. By night he rises from his grave to wander through the village, making fearful sounds. Everyone is afraid to go about after dusk. No one goes outside alone at night... not even to the woodpile! I'll have you know that even our boldest men are afraid of this warlock!"

"I'm not," Timofey said plainly, with no trace of bravado. In Timofey's mind, his utterance was simply a statement of fact.

"How could even you not fear a warlock? You've only a sword... and that might mean little in battle with a warlock."

"Do you recall the old saying," continued the young warrior, "'Crown property cannot be drowned or burned in fire.'? Well, you know that I am crown property, therefore I must modestly tell you that no warlock will scare me."

With that proclamation still ringing in Zaretski's ears, he watched Timofey, now walking, become a distant shadow, soon disappearing into the enveloping haze that hung by the churchyard.

As Timofey neared the rusted, iron gate that once served the graveyard, he noted that the latch was broken and could no longer be closed. Then something else caught his eye. In a back corner of the property, among the most remote gravestones, there was a bright fire blazing.

"What's this," he asked himself. "I'll have a look."

He walked among the slabs of chiseled rock that marked the resting places of his ancestors and other deceased townspeople.

As he neared the far corner of the field, he spied the warlock, sitting by the fire, mending his boots. Timofey called.

"Hello, Brother!"

The warlock barely raised his eyes.

"Why are you here, soldier? This is no battleground."

"Of course not, Comrade. I only wanted to see what you were doing."

The warlock was silent for long moments, while he finished his mending. He bit through the thread and laid aside the needle, before standing. Once erect, his hellish features became almost menacing; but Timofey stood, unwavering.

"Alright," snapped the warlock. "You want to see what I'm doing? Then come along. We're going to a wedding party, so that we can have some fun! Try to keep pace!"

As the warlock walked in a different direction than Timofey had been heading, it became obvious that the warlock was going to a neighboring town; not that of Timofey's family. Timofey, proud of his strenuous training, pushed to stay walking beside the warlock, who seemed especially eager to get to the festive event.

Once arrived at the wedding party, the unquestioning hosts offered the new arrivals drinks and foods worthy of the special occasion. While Timofey watched, the warlock downed several mugs of vodka and wine, before suddenly turning surly and fearsome. He began menacing everyone with his grimace and his groans. Then he chased all the guests from the grounds. He then turned to terrifying both bride and groom until they fainted from fright.

As the curious soldier observed, the warlock removed two tiny objects from a coat pocket. They were miniature glass bottles; one tinted and one clear. He also withdrew a sharply-pointed awl from another pocket. He proceeded to stab each of the unconscious newlyweds in the palm of the right hand, catching some of their blood in the small containers, which he jammed deep into his coat pockets. Now smiling wickedly, he turned to his companion.

"Well, let's be off. It was a grand party!"

Timofey, outwardly calm, was barely able to talk; but managed to quietly ask the warlock,

"Tell me, why did you draw off some blood and collect it in those vessels?"

"Why? It's very simple. By tomorrow they will have died and will be joining me in Death." He continued, sneering, "I lack companionship since I entered the grave... aside from an occasional idiot or simpleton soldier who wanders into my domain!"

Timofey, becoming more concerned for his own safety, was silent; but the warlock couldn't keep from boasting.

"Happily, they will remain in the world of the dead, since I'm the only one who knows how to restore life to the bride and groom."

"How do you manage that, Comrade? Do you mind telling me?"

"Of course I don't mind telling someone like you... a fool warrior who has neither a musket nor a horse! Besides, it is simple reasoning... reverse the procedure! I simply puncture a heel of each of my future companions and replace some of the lost blood. Its very reliable. And you see, here is the groom's blood in this tinted vial and the bride's blood is in the clear one."

Timofey listened closely. His mind grasped every word that came from the bragging warlock, who was enjoying his chance to boast freely of his powers.

"Further, there's not much that I can't do if I've a mind to do it."

"How fascinating," gushed Timofey, "that no one can ever get the best of you."

"Oh, I'm sure one could... if they only knew the secret and if they also had the will. But no one does."

After a moment, he continued.

"And if they did learn the secret, I'd simply kill them anyway."

Timofey and his evil companion walked in silence for a while, until Timofey sorted his thoughts, trying to figure a way to combat all the wickedness he'd seen.

"Since I suppose that you plan to kill me anyway, Comrade, would you mind telling me that secret, so that I could at least die with the feeling that I'd learned something unique while on this earth?"

"Since you already know your fate, warrior, and since you accept it, I don't mind telling you what you ask. However, I must say that even if one were to try it, and make it through the first step, he'd never get through the second..."

The warlock paused momentarily before launching into his explanation of what could rob him of his ghoulish powers.

"One would need to gather aspen logs and boughs... by the wagon load... even by the dozens of wagon loads... about a hundred wagon loads ! Then he'd need to set them afire of course and toss me on top of the funeral pyre... and that would be the easy part; because, once I am on the fire, the exciting part begins!"

While the warlock paused, before relating the second vital step in the process, Timofey rehashed the process in his own mind. Thus, very quickly, he was again ready to focus on the self-assured warlock's vivid recipe for his own destruction.

"My great strength, tin soldier, unlike you and your fellow townspeople, is this: While you are single individuals... I contain legions. I hold a host of living beings... insects, worms, birds, and so forth. Therefore, when my body is burned and opens, a hundred life forms will emerge and it simply requires one escaping being to survive, for me to re-emerge. Just one!" he concluded.

Again, inwardly Timofey cringed in disgust and fear; but he had already created the jeopardy to himself that he must now try to avoid. However, unrecognized by the swaggering warlock, Timofey Pavlovitch Kalganov had the will.

Suddenly, the warlock, declared, "I'm home!"

The startled Timofey looked about himself. He was standing beside the grave of the warlock. He glanced at the cold ashes that were the residue of the fire that had earlier drawn his attention to the warlock. Instinctively, his hand gripped the handle of his sword.

"Now," shouted the swaggering warlock, "I am going to rip you to shreds!"

The stillness of the graveyard was broken by the loud gnashing of teeth. The soldier looked intently at the warlock. He watched the warlock move into an animal-like crouch. His grip on his sword handle tightened; but he made no move, wanting to wait for the exact moment for pulling the steel blade from its sheath.

The warlock sprang. The blade was just as suddenly cutting the air between the mortal enemies.

The warlock stopped in his tracks, surprised at the soldier's skillful move. Realizing that he would have to avoid the sword, and not yet aware of Tomofey's ability, the warlock stepped backward.

Timofey knew only that he had been diligent in his study of fencing. He knew that he had out-dueled his army instructor to become the best swordsman at their outpost. Now, he must employ every skill he had learned, and perhaps quickly acquire some new ones, if he was to survive this beastly attack!

Timofey soon learned that his vicious opponent was very agile and very speedy. Timofey also realized that if the warlock got closer than the sword's point, he would keep his promise to rip the brave warrior to bits! The deadly combat raged.

As hours passed, the wearying Timofey saw that —so long as his energy and speed lasted—he could keep the warlock away; but he also noted that he had not been able to get the sword's point to its mark: the warlock's body. His own energy was waning. He was struggling for breath. The situation finally reached the point where Timofey could count the seconds before he would slip or fall to one knee or simply collapse. Whichever happened, it would be the warlock's bloody triumph!

Timofey made several desperate lunges at the warlock, who stepped aside for each. Timofey's arm could no longer lift the weight of his sword. The arm dropped, the sword dangling, its point resting on the earth, on the spot that should soon become the warrior's grave...

Somewhere in the distance, a rooster crowed... then others.

Timofey, hearing the sound, staggered backward, still expecting the deadly attack. However, before his startled eyes, the warlock just as suddenly collapsed into a heap at Timofey's feet. The arrival of a bright new day had saved the soldier!

After resting briefly, Timofey removed the two glass vials from the warlock's pocket and proceeded to walk to his village and to his parent's house. Friends also quickly collected at the house to see their returned neighbor. A young boy called,

"Were you in any battles?"

"No, my young comrade. Our portion of the frontier was always quiet."

From an older man, "Did you see any excitement on your journey home?"

"No more than usual, I suppose," said the modest corporal, who then asked a question of those near him.

"Was there a wedding in one of the neighboring towns recently?"

All spoke at once, so that Timofey could barely grasp what they were excitedly trying to relate. Still Timofey, who already knew the situation, could hear them declaring that a marriage had, indeed, occurred, but that the young bride and groom had both died during the night. No one knew why. Speculation was that both had caught a deadly illness, or both had been poisoned, or that some other horrible calamity had struck just the two hapless newlyweds.

In a strong clear voice, Timofey thanked all who had come to welcome his return. Then he announced, very clearly, that they should return to their homes and let him quench his thirst and hunger. Then he would sleep briefly, before going to the scene of the tragedy. He felt confident, he told the incredulous crowd, that he could help restore the couple's lives.

After dozing for little more than a nap, Timofey began his walk to the neighboring town. As he departed from his own village, many of his family and townspeople joined him, doubtful that he could be of any service to the lost souls or their families; but curious to see what he was planning.

Timofey asked the first villager whom he met, as he entered the town: "Where are the bodies of the dead bride and groom being held?"

"The corpses were both taken to the house of the groom's father. It's on the right, just beyond the cooperage."

The groom's father was the district's largest landowner and his house was the finest in the village. As Timofey drew closer he saw that the crowd, without counting those who had arrived with him, was already spilling into the street. He pushed through the throng and through the door.

Once inside the house, Timofey sought the father, pulled him aside and declared: "I know how to bring this young couple to life again. What will you offer if I do?"

"I believe, Soldier, that you have lost your senses; but I'll gleefully give you half of my wealth if you restore their lives!"

Timofey then followed the instructions that he'd been given by the warlock. He punctured a heel of each and took the blood from its containers and returned it to the bodies from which it had been stolen by the warlock. It was as though they had merely slept. Both opened their eyes, smiled at those around them and greeted the soldier, although both said that they couldn't remember his being invited to their wedding.

The soldier was treated as the hero he was. The groom's father greeted his newly restored son as if he'd been gone for years, and then he created the documents needed to share his wealth with Timofey.

Timofey wished the couple a long and happy marriage before he started for his own village. As soon as he arrived, he told the townspeople of his churchyard encounter with the warlock and why he had been able to restore the lives of the newlyweds. Then he ordered them to bring a hundred loads of aspen boughs and logs to the warlock's grave. He also told them to bring shovels, brooms and the iron pokers used in tending their fires.

Once all had arrived, the aspen was piled into a huge heap, on top of which the warlock's body was placed. As Timofey had instructed, all stood close, ready to act. As the fire blazed higher, the warlock's body roasted and burst. Lizards, snakes, and worms crawled from the corpse, while blackbirds and magpies flew from inside the warlock's burning body. Timofey and all his companions crushed and burned every form of life that emerged from the body, down to the last maggot, before Timofey gathered the ashes and scattered them into the evening wind.

Timofey visited with his family until his furlough was nearly ended. He then sent a note for one-tenth of his new fortune as a wedding gift to the newlyweds; gave his family half of his remaining wealth; bought a stout, young draft horse and started back to his military post. His first stop was with the miller, who was given the strong, young draft horse, and from whom Timofey regained his own riding horse on which to return to his military post.

Years later, when his military service ended, Timofey returned to his own village, to enjoy his years of retirement as the honored and respected veteran who had once given new life to a weary, warlock-haunted village.

The Fifteenth Skazka

MOTHER FRIDAY

In some cultures, the days of the week were personified. That is, a day was recognized as having human traits. Such a one in old Russia was Mother Friday. It was believed by many that Mother Friday wandered about the huts of the peasantry of old Russia. It was understood that Mother Friday had certain chores that she did not want people to perform on a Friday. Men were not expected to twine cord or make cord shoes, among other things. Similarly, women were not expected to sew, spin threads or weave cloth.   All understood that Mother Friday found the dust from their work to be very annoying. Those who respected that belief would not perform those chores on that day of the week. The peasant woman, Raisa, was one of the naughty exceptions.

Raisa didn't pay proper respect to Mother Friday. Instead of remaining worshipful to Mother Friday, she spent the day working on a distaff of flax. She spent much of the day spinning and whirling the flax. As dinner time approached, she was still working. Suddenly, Raisa dozed, falling into a deep sleep.

Suddenly, the cottage door opened and in rushed Mother Friday, clad in a fine white dress and all in a rage! The others who were in the room shied away from Mother Friday. After looking directly at each cowering person in the room, Mother Friday stepped over to the sleeping Raisa. Poor Raisa didn't even awaken, while Mother Friday scooped up a large handful of the dust that had fallen from the flax, and piled it unto Raisa's eyes. Then Mother Friday hurried from the cottage.

When Raisa finally awakened, she rubbed at her eyes and moaned and squealed at the top of her lungs. She had no idea what had happened to her eyes! Blinded by the flax dust, Raisa was unable to open them or to see about! The other women, still shaking with fright, cried out, "Oh, wretch. You've brought a terrible punishment on yourself from Mother Friday!"

Then the other women told Raisa all that had taken place while she slept. She listened intently to every word of chiding from the other women. Then the blinded Raisa began loudly wailing:

"Mother Friday, please forgive me," she implored. "Please pardon my behavior. I'm the guilty one!"

Raisa continued, "Dear Mother Friday, I'll burn a taper for thee tonight... and I'll never let anyone, friend or foe, dishonor thee in my presence!"

That very night, Mother Friday returned to Raisa's cottage. She removed the dust from the eyes of poor Raisa.

The peasant woman, Raisa, had suffered for her disrespect; but from that day onward, all the residents of the town became more passionate in their show of respect for Mother Friday. No longer did the womenfolk or the menfolk of the village dishonor Mother Friday by doing any Friday combing and spinning of flax, forsooth [to be truthful]!

The Sixteenth Skazka:

THE WITCH OF DEATH

Darkness had already descended on the village of Oboyan when Emelian, a Cossack, rode into the village and pulled up at the last cottage on the street, close to the river's bank. The Cossacks were noted cavalry soldiers who lived near, and defended, Russia's southern border. Emelian shouted to the inhabitants of the cottage, "Hello.... Will you let me spend the night here?"

He heard a clear voice reply, "Come in, if you are unafraid of Death."

The Cossack was filled with wonder. "What sort of a reply is that?" he thought, while leading his horse to the stable. So, returning to the cottage, he pushed open the heavy door and entered.

Within the cottage a number of men, women and children were seated. All were sobbing and lamenting, while offering sorrowful prayers to God. Emelian, the Cossack, watched in silence. He saw them get control of their sobbing and then they began putting on clean shirts. Now, he spoke again.

"Why is everyone crying?"

Although the sobbing had become more subdued, they were still whimpering, as the master of the house spoke.

"You see, Warrior, at night Death stalks our village. And whichever house she looks into, all the inhabitants of the house die... every member. On the following day, after she visits, all the inhabitants of the house are hauled away to the graveyard." After pausing, he concluded, "Tonight it is our turn."

Emelian declared, "Never fear, master! Without God's will, no pig gets its fill!"

But, none listened to his reassuring comment. Instead, they pulled their blankets tight around themselves and fell asleep.

Emelian, however, stayed alert. He propped himself against an outer wall, far from the huge stove. He wanted to remain awake and felt that the further he sat from the heat, the more alert he would be. He was fighting sleepiness when, at exactly midnight, Emelian heard a window being opened. He saw, dressed all in white, the Witch of Death. He watched closely while the witch took a sprinkler and began shaking it. Before she could release much of her deadly powder, Emelian unsheathed his sabre and swung it.

The witch's arm was severed completely and fell to the floor! The killer witch shrieked and squealed like a dog as she ran away. Emelian, the Cossack, picked up the fallen limb and wiped the bloody end, as well as the blood on the floor. Then he slipped the arm into his jacket and, very exhausted from his encounter, he finally fell asleep.

The next morning, the master and the mistress of the house awakened. In the near darkness of the early dawn, they quickly peered about, looking at the other family members, all of whom were moving about. The master and his wife were dumbfounded to find that everyone was alive.

The master awakened their Cossack guest.

"What have you done? How did you save us?"

"Come," said Emelian, "I'll show you the Witch of Death. But, first, gather all the local constables and do it quickly. Then we'll go through the village and find the witch." They soon returned with a half-dozen local police.

Although very uneasy with the prospect of facing Death, the members of the surviving family gingerly followed the Cossack and police. They moved from house to house, through the village. In each house, Emelian asked the parents, "Are all of your family members present?"

In each house, in turn, all family members appeared.

Finally, Emelian, the Cossack, led his group to the Mar's cottage. [A Mar, or Ponomar, was similar to a church sexton.] Again, Emelian inquired, "Are all of your family members present?"

The distraught sexton and his wife, blurted, "Yes, we're all here; but our one daughter is horribly ill... she's over there, resting on the stove." [Note: Many Russian stoves were designed so that people could sleep on top of them on cold nights.]

All present looked at the stove. There was the sexton's daughter, lying ill and with a thick and bloody bandage on the stump of her arm, a short distance from her shoulder!

The Cossack carefully related all that had occurred and, at the end of his account, he pulled the severed arm from within his jacket. Thereupon, the constables removed the witch from the cottage. The witch was sentenced to be drowned, while the villagers soon gathered some money to reward Emelian the Cossack.

The Seventeenth Skazka

THE TWO CORPSES

Stepan was a loyal soldier who had obtained leave to return to his home, so that he might pray to the holy images and to bow down before his parents. As night fell and the country road became devoid of other travelers, Stepan found himself walking past an isolated churchyard. As he was passing a small family chapel, he was attracted to the chapel doorway because of the candle light that brightened that doorway. In that instant, he heard a shout directly behind him.

"Stop, soldier! You can't escape!"

He looked behind himself to see a corpse, running very fast and gnashing his teeth. Suddenly becoming very alert, Stepan leaped aside just as the corpse was set to snare him. Now in a mood of panic, the terrified solder leaped into the small chapel. He shuddered as he saw that the only thing in the chapel with him was a second corpse that was lying on a stone table. Tapers that were burning for the corpse were also the source of light that drew Stepan's attention to the chapel in the first place.

The terrified soldier crouched in a corner as far from the doorway as he could hide. Stepan didn't look up when he heard a noise, although he was sure it was his ghastly pursuer, coming directly into the chapel in order to find Stepan.

At that moment, the corpse on the table arose. As Stepan peeked at the scene, the corpse that had been on the table confronted the other corpse.

93

"Why hast thou burst into my chapel?"

The other answered. "I've chased a soldier into this chapel. I'm going to catch him and devour him!"

"Oh, no, Brother. That soldier has run into my chapel. He will be my supper!"

"No, no, no. I saw him first. I chased him. He shall be my supper!"

"No, Brother. He will be my supper!"

With no more words, they attacked one another.

Dust flew as they clawed and bit and kicked! Their shrieking voices grew ever so much louder.

Stepan remained cowering. He felt hopeless. No matter which corpse won the fight, the eventual winner would dine on Stepan's mortal flesh. Oh, how he wished that it was all over. He sobbed and slunk even deeper into the corner where he had been trying to hide.

The historic battle of the private chapel waged on and on. Meanwhile, the soldier over whom the battle was being waged had lost all sense of time and place. He was a simpering fool, with no place to turn. They'd have gone on fighting ever so much longer; but the crowing of a rooster brought a halt to the fight and the ghouls dropped, lifeless, to the cold earth. The terrified Stepan stared at the lifeless pair for several minutes, fearful that they would jump up again, animated and ready to rip his young body to shreds. At last, Stepan grasped the good fortune that he had been given. He kept wary eyes on both corpses until he was several steps away, then he turned and walked resolutely toward home, with many sighs of relief and with a thankful prayer:

"Glory be to Thee, O' Lord! Thank you for saving me from those ravenous ghouls."

The Eighteenth Skazka

THE WOODLAND DAMSEL

Oksana, a priest's daughter, loved the forest. One day, without asking permission of either of her parents, she decided to stroll into the forest. As the sun sank and dusk arrived, she had not yet returned. One of her brothers told their parents that he had seen her enter the forest, walking alone and cheerful. Despite their repeated calls, she did not reply. Nor did she return the next day, or the next. Groups of relatives and fellow villagers formed search parties; but found nothing. After anxious searches, the hunt was suspended. Perhaps she was a victim of wild animals, some reasoned. Although her parents often journeyed into the forest, they never found even a trace of Oksana. Of course, the forest in that region was huge and dense. Even those who hunted and trapped in that terrain sometimes got lost. In fact, three years passed and she hadn't come home.

In the same commune there lived a young nimrod whose name was Rodion. Daily, he took his dog and his gun and went into the forest. Still a young man who lived with his parents and siblings, hunting was Rodion's livelihood. He, too, had aided in the hunt for Oksana and it was Rodion who finally told the people that such a search was hopeless. The forest was far greater than their small numbers could explore. Because of Rodion's reputation as a hunter and man of the forest, the villagers had reluctantly abandoned their search.

Rodion had named his dog, Sirius, in honor of the dog in a story he had heard about a skillful Greek hunter, Orion. The dog was an excellent hunting companion. Thus, at daybreak, one autumn day, Rodion took his dog, Sirius, and his gun and entered the forest, planning to get game to feed his own parents and siblings and with enough remaining to gain a rouble or two. Today, he was even deeper into the forest than he normally walked. By mid-morning, he had killed a couple of hares, gutted them and stuffed them into the deep pockets of his hunting jacket. Still walking in unfamiliar terrain, Rodion came to the edge of a small clearing. There he saw a young woman sitting on a log and repairing a shoe made of bast, (plant fibers from the inner bark of Linden and other trees). As a hunter who was used to quietly observing his prey, Rodion watched, fascinated. Sirius, Rodian's hunting companion, was well trained. He, too, stood quietly beside his master. The maiden appeared to be organized and competent; but her clothes were tattered and rotting, with little wear remaining. Her garments were also ill fitting, suggesting that they were long outgrown.

Eventually, the young woman looked up from her work. She was startled by the stranger and she quickly dropped her shoe and darted into the thicket. Rodion called after the fleeing maiden, "Wait, I'll not harm you." However, she didn't wait and, in a trice, she was gone from view.

Rodion did not dash after her. Again, his hunting instincts dictated his behavior. He knew that his dog could track the damsel and he didn't want to add to her fright by any quick pursuit. Instead he picked up her fallen shoe, marveling at the natural skill of its maker. Then he took a leash from his belt. He tied the leash around the dog's neck and kept the animal at a walking pace as it tracked his feminine quarry.

Beside a swift-flowing rill, Rodion saw a small, rude cabin. Unknown to him, the rough structure was an abandoned trapper's shack, apparently claimed by the young woman who was missing a shoe. Staying hidden among the trees, Rodion watched to assess the scene. There was no movement that he could detect until twilight descended on the forest. Then he saw the maiden open the door of the tiny cabin. She peered out first and, seeing nothing of concern, she stepped out, carrying a wooden pail. She walked to the brook and held the pail in the stream until it filled. Then she returned to the shack. As she stepped inside, she was startled by the presence of the hunter, who pushed shut the door behind her, so that she was trapped within with the armed stranger.

With the gentlest of moves, Rodion handed her the fallen bast shoe. Then he gently asked if she might prepare some food for him. Although only slightly reassured of her safety, she moved to a cupboard and brought him a dish containing uncooked plant roots. He recognized the roots as some that he had often eaten while in the forest. Next, Rodion poured a cup of water into the pot that hung in the small fireplace. Then he kindled a fire beneath the pot. He then drew the hares from his coat, skinned them quickly, cut them into pieces and added them to the pot. He added her plant roots to the stew. He noticed a tin container on the mantle. It likely held salt; but had been empty for months. When the savory hares were ready, he put some of the food on a plate for himself and some on a plate for the maiden. As he was sitting on the only chair in the shack, she sat on a wooden crate by the fireplace, still eyeing him suspiciously. However, she seemed delighted to have meat with her meal. Surely, Oksana had forgotten the robust flavor of wild game, properly cooked.

Rodion, for his part, was surveying the contents of a trapper's once-temporary lodging. The current occupant, the young damsel, had learned the ways of the forest. He saw that she had cut and gathered enough firewood to heat the cabin for the coming winter season.

Some spring-blooming wildflowers, now dry and brown, were displayed in a rusting can.

The trapper, who may not have used this cabin for years, had left a tattered jacket and a pair of well-worn boots; all of which must have served this female hermit. There were several iron traps hanging on a wooden peg on the one wall; but they, too, may not have been used for years.

At some point, Rodion had a revelation. This dark-eyed young woman, despite her disheveled and nearly wild appearance, was attractive as well. And, when his gun slid to the floor, noisily, as he tried in vain to grab it, she smiled. He also found her smile to be especially appealing.

Believing that he had been patient long enough to make her feel secure, he addressed her gently.

"What is your name?"

She frowned and gave a negative shake of her head. Rodion was convinced that she didn't know her name.

"And who are your parents?"

Again, there was no sign of recognition.

"Where was your home?"

Once more, she looked puzzled. "I can't recall. I know that I came from the rocky creek bottom, where I must have fallen. That's when I happened upon this cabin."

Rodion was now convinced that this maiden had fallen or was otherwise injured while in the forest and, while trying to adjust to her environment, became a child of the forest.

Rodion slowly explained to the damsel that she must have come from his village and that her parents had long searched for her. Her name, he suggested gently, was Oksana. His descriptions of the village and her family and her home seemed to stir her imagination. In the morning, he promised, they would walk to the village and she could see if he might be correct in his assessments. His way of declaring their destination: "Tomorrow, I will take you back to Holy Russia."

Rodion and Sirius slept on the bare plank floor while the young woman, who had claimed the tiny cabin as her home several years earlier, used the trapper's rough-hewn cot.

At daybreak, Rodion and his new companion ate a few of the plants that she had earlier gathered. As they walked from the hut, small songbirds circled them. She slowed her step and spoke softly to them, as she must have done on many other mornings. Then she hurried to join Rodion and Sirius as they walked the many versts to the village.

As the hunter and his companion walked through the streets, the news preceded them. The priest and his wife came running from their cottage. "That," beamed the priest, "is our daughter… our dear Oksana!" His tearful wife was even more enthusiastic.

"Oh, my dear child! Where have you been for so long? I thought that I would never see you again."

Oksana just blinked her eyes, understanding nothing.

As the weeks passed, she slowly regained her senses. Then the priest and his wife gave her in marriage to Rodion. They also rewarded him with all sorts of good things.

Although townspeople often walked into the forest, looking for the trapper's cabin, the fabled hut by the brook was never found.

The Nineteenth Skazka

There are, in the world of opera, a number of truly famous operas by the Italian composer, Giacomo Puccini (1858-1924). Among his best-known works is the opera entitled "Turandot."

The story to which Puccini attached the music, tells of a lovely Chinese princess, Turandot. She seems to be opposed to getting married, since she has been using a system for choosing a mate that nearly condemns her to spinsterhood. Her system was to have suitors answer her three riddles. Should the suitor answer her three riddles, she would marry him. However, if a suitor failed to guess all three, he was executed, by beheading! Here, again, the reader will encounter, in the Russian culture, a very similar story.

THE BLIND MAN AND THE CRIPPLE

In one of the early Russian kingdoms, there lived a prince named Ivan. His parents, the king and queen, had appointed a mentor or tutor to teach and guide their young prince. The tutor's name was Katoma. When the parents neared death, they summoned Ivan into their presence. Here was a major element of their parting advice:

"When we are dead, accept the advice of Katoma in all that you do. Should you listen to Katoma and follow his advice, you will prosper. But, if you disobey him, you will quickly perish like a fly."

The king and queen died the very next day. Prince Ivan buried his parents with a loving ceremony. He then began living as he knew they would have advised. Whatever he needed to do, he first consulted Katoma.

After several years, Ivan attained adulthood. He approached his tutor, complaining, "I'm tired of living alone. I wish to marry."

"Well, Prince Ivan. There is nothing to prevent your marrying, once you find a partner. So, go into the great hall and there you'll find portraits of many prospective brides... princesses from all over the world. Find the portrait of the one that pleases you and we'll send a marriage proposal."

Ivan went to the great hall, where he soon found a marvel of beauty. Her name was Anna the Fair. Beneath her portrait, however, was this note:

"If a suitor asks Anna the Fair a riddle and she can't answer it, she will marry the riddler/suitor. However, should she guess the riddle, that suitor will be beheaded."

Upset by what he read, Ivan reported this development to his tutor.

Katoma's reaction was not encouraging. "Yes, Prince Ivan, Anna the Fair is beautiful, to be sure; but she may be difficult to win. You'll never win her without help; but if you take me along, and do exactly as I instruct you, the affair may be managed."

Prince Ivan promised Katoma that, if Katoma accompanied him, he'd do exactly as Katoma advised.

The prince and his mentor prepared for the journey to a far distant land. They traveled for a year, then a second year. Only after three years of travel did they reach the kingdom where Anna the Fair resided. Ivan lamented to Katoma, "We've traveled for three long years and crossed many mountains, rivers and borders. But, we still have not thought of a riddle for me to propound in order to win her.

"We shall manage to think of one in good time," Katoma assured him.

Shortly thereafter, Katoma was looking down at the road and saw, lying there, a purse full of money. He lifted the purse and poured all the money from the purse into his own purse. So he said:

"Here's a riddle for you, Prince Ivan: When you come into the presence of the princess, propound a riddle to her in these words:

'As we were coming along, we saw Good lying on the road. We took up the Good with Good, and placed it in our own Good!'

"That riddle," Katoma continued, "she won't guess in a lifetime; but any other one she would find out quickly. She would only have to look into her magic book, and as soon as she had guessed it, she'd order your head to be cut off."

Well, at last Prince Ivan and his tutor arrived at the lofty palace in which dwelt the haughty Anna the Fair. At that very moment, the princess was on a balcony and saw their arrival. She sent to inquire as to their purpose. Prince Ivan replied,

"I have come from my own kingdom, far, far to the west. I petition for the hand of Princess Anna the Fair."

She quickly set a meeting with Ivan before the princes and boyars of her council. There, with Prince Ivan as the guest, she repeated the rules of her challenge.

"Listen to my riddle, fair princess," declared Prince Ivan. "As we came toward your kingdom, I saw Good lying on the road and we took up the Good with Good and placed it in our own Good."

Princess Anna the Fair began leafing through her magic book; but could find no answer to his riddle. So the Princess and her boyars decided that the Princess must marry Prince Ivan. She was not at all pleased to have lost; but began to prepare for the wedding.

In the meantime, she decided, she would try to delay things and try to overwhelm the groom with daunting chores. However, every chore she asked him to do, brought his indignant reply: "Excuse me, Princess, but I'm not here for such and such a task. I have a servant, Katoma, to do that sort of thing."

Each time, the princess would be stifled in her effort to destroy Prince Ivan by heavy chores, as Katoma performed them in Ivan's place. So the marriage took place, with the princess scheming and privately damning Katoma for thwarting her plans! And for the first year of their marriage, she constantly complained about Katoma; but Prince Ivan would not discharge his tutor, who was also his loyal protector. Her condemnations only made Prince Ivan feel more and more sympathy for Katoma.

At the end of their first year of marriage, Prince Ivan said to Princess Anna the Fair, "Beautiful Princess, my beloved spouse! I would like to take you to see my own kingdom."

"By all means, let us go, my prince. I've been hoping to see your kingdom."

They gathered their goods and climbed into the carriage, which was driven by Katoma.

When Prince Ivan finally dozed, in the carriage, Princess Anna the Fair, created this ruse: She awakened Prince Ivan and berated him, "Listen, Prince. You're always sleeping and you hear nothing. Your tutor defies every order that I give. He drives us so recklessly that it seems that he wants to kill us both! I can't live like this! You must punish Katoma!"

Poor Prince Ivan, still half asleep, handed his tutor over to the princess, blurting, "Deal with him as you wish."

Princess Anna the Fair ordered her servants to cut off Katoma's feet! This was promptly done. Then she ordered her servants to hoist the sobbing Katoma to the top of a tall tree stump, so that he was utterly stranded. She then had Prince Ivan tethered to the carriage, so that he had to run hard to keep up with the carriage which was now, under Princess Anna's orders, driving back to her own kingdom!

Prince Ivan, running and stumbling behind her carriage, realized his stupid blunder; but had no way to correct it. So, as soon as they were back in her kingdom, Princess Anna assigned Prince Ivan the job of cow herder. He was ordered to drive the herd to the pastures each morning and to drive them back into the royal yard each evening. When he returned with the herd, his spouse was always sitting on the balcony and counting, to be sure that Prince Ivan lost none of the herd.

Meanwhile, Katoma remained seated on the stump, unable to get down or to go anywhere or get anything to eat or drink. Days went by, with him still condemned to the stump. Unknown to Katoma, there lived in a hut within a nearby forest, a once-mighty hero, Viktor, who was now blind. His unique way of getting food was to crouch in a field. When he smelled the approach of an animal, whether it was a fox, rabbit or even a bear, he quickly gave chase. Viktor could outrun any of these animals and was able to get his next meal. Now it happened, that on this day, he was in pursuit of a fox. The fearful beast ran at top speed, but Viktor was gaining. The fox ran straight toward a stump, then took a sudden turn. Poor Viktor, the sightless hero, ran smack into that stump with his head! He hit it with such force that the impact knocked the stump from the ground. Katoma fell from the stump to the ground. Lying there, sprawled, he asked the blind one, "Who are you?"

Viktor identified himself and told his own harrowing tale. He had been blinded on orders of the accursed Princess Anna the Fair. The two men talked for hours and finally agreed to combine their skills for the good of both. Viktor, the blind man, carried Katoma on his back. Katoma, in turn, advised Viktor on where to go to get their game and so on.

One day the blind Viktor observed, "I've heard that in the village beyond the forest there is a rich merchant, who has a lovely daughter, named Zoya. That daughter, folks say, is exceedingly kind and gives alms to the poor. Perhaps Zoya would come and live with us and keep house for us.

Their plan was really a plot. They drove a cart into the village and into the merchant's courtyard. When Zoya saw them, she came into the courtyard and offered them a coin. Katoma reached for the coin; but grabbed her wrist and pulled her into the cart. With Viktor driving, they sped out of town, traveling far too fast for anyone to catch them.

Once they were back in the hut, the cripple and the blind man spoke to Zoya.

"Please stay here with us. Be like a sister to us. Otherwise, we'll have no one to cook our meals or wash our shirts... God won't desert you if you do this!"

Zoya agreed to do this; but only if they could let her return to inform her father. They put her back in the cart and drove back into town. When the merchant saw them, he fumed. He threatened to have them arrested and quartered; but Zoya dissuaded him and convinced him that she wanted to use the opportunity to help two people who were truly in need. So the irate merchant became the understanding father. He gave Zoya some supplies and sent them on their way.

Zoya remained with the needy couple. They respected her, loved her and accepted her as a sister. Through extreme good fortune, the two men happened upon a woodland spring that had healing powers. Viktor tried some of its waters on his eyes and his sight returned. So he quickly lifted his compatriot and sank Katoma's legs into the water. Katoma's feet returned to normal.

Now restored to full health, they had things to do. Katoma professed his love for Zoya. She reciprocated. They were soon married in a solemn, but joyous ceremony in the church of Zoya's father.

Then the three traveled to the kingdom of Princess Anna the Fair. At the edge of the capital city, Katoma spied his bedraggled friend, Prince Ivan, driving a herd of cows. Katoma called,

"Stop, herdsman! Where are you driving those cows?"

The prince, not recognizing his former tutor, tried to answer.

"I'm driving them to the courtyard of the Princess. She will be waiting to see that every cow is counted."

"Here, herdsman. Take my clothes and put them on, and I will put on your clothes and drive the cows back to the courtyard."

Prince Ivan was quick to disagree. "No. No, brother. That cannot be done. If the Princess found out, she'd be a raging fury!"

"Never fear, Prince. Nothing will happen. Katoma will guarantee that."

The prince's laugh was hollow. "Hah, good man. If only Katoma were alive... I would not be herding these beasts."

Katoma then revealed who he was and all that had happened. Prince Ivan warmly hugged Katoma and burst into tears. "I was sure that I'd never see you again."

They exchanged clothes and Katoma drove the cattle into the courtyard, beneath the princess who was watching from a balcony. As Anna the Fair watched, all but one of the cows went into the sheds. Katoma, still unrecognized by the princess, shouted at the lingering cow:

"What are you waiting for, dog's meat!"

Katoma then grabbed the sluggish cow by its tail. He pulled so hard that he pulled its entire skin from the cow!

Princess Anna shouted, "What is that stupid cowherd doing? Seize him and bring him to me!"

Servants grabbed Katoma, who offered no resistance, and took him before the angry princess.

The princess glared at him, "Who are you and where do you come from?"

"I am the man whose feet you had cut off and whom you had placed on a tall stump!

My name is Katoma. Katoma. KATOMA!"

The visitor stunned her so thoroughly that she suddenly realized her utter foolishness. She apologized to Katoma and begged his forgiveness. As Zoya, Viktor and Prince Ivan walked onto the scene, Princess Anna offered intense apologies to Viktor and swore to Prince Ivan that she would be his obedient wife, henceforth. The prince and princess, she vowed, would rule as co-equals, for the good of every single one of their subjects.

Amazing as it may seem, the power of her former enemies wrought a genuine change in Princess Anna the Fair.

Viktor was appointed to an important ministerial post with the Prince and Princess, while Katoma and Zoya returned to the home of her rich merchant father and took up their abode under his roof.

The Twentieth Skazka

THE IMMORTAL KOSHCHEI

As any serious scholar would admit, Eurasia is a singular continent, with the great cultural center, Europe, being but an appendage of the greater land mass to the east. Not only are the peoples of Eurasia united on the same bit of land; but there are cultural strains that often bind them. There are many examples to offer as proof of these cultural tethers. Their folklore is but one such tie.

It should also be noted that there is a large fish, the pike, appearing in this tale. The pike, with its great size and its mouth full of sharp teeth, has a common presence in northern folk tales.

The Russian Koshchei (pronounced KOSS chay) has counterparts in several other lands. He had a frightening demeanor. His every glance was a glare that could frighten children. Even more disturbing, his glance could frighten adults, as well. He was just slightly taller than the tallest members of the community; but his face – gnarled and grotesque as it was – made people shudder when he returned their stare. Far more frightening than his appearance, was his activity. He commonly kidnapped innocent folk. Even more frightening: Koshchei was deathless. What could further encourage wicked behavior in a wicked being than the knowledge that he, or she, was deathless? Koshchei reveled in his immortality. Added to his list of traits, he had the ability to fly.

One kidnapping victim of Koshchei was Inessa, the queen of a modest Russian kingdom. Inessa and King Pavel were the parents to three adult sons. By age, the princes were named Illarion, Veniamin, and Ivan. When Koshchei kidnapped their mother, the eldest son, Illarion, requested his father's blessing so that he could seek his imprisoned mother. With the king's blessing assured, the eldest son departed to seek his mother; but Prince Illarion vanished. The middle son then secured the king's blessing. When that blessing was obtained, Veniamin went to find his mother. He too disappeared. This second failure led to the decision by the youngest son, Ivan, to try to rescue his mother.

For the third son, the king refused to give his blessing. "I cannot give you my blessing. I've lost two sons already. Should I lose you, I would die of grief!"

"But, Father. If you bless me, I shall go. If you refuse to bless me, I shall still go."

With little choice, King Pavel gave his paternal blessing to Ivan.

The prince, we must tell you, had superhuman strength. This made finding a steed to his liking to be nearly impossible. As Ivan walked through the stable, every horse on which he placed his hand, sank beneath the prince's strength. This led the prince to wander along the roadway, pondering his next move.

Suddenly Larisa, an elderly woman appeared. When Prince Ivan glanced at her, she inquired,

"Why are you so sad, Prince Ivan?"

The interruption angered him.

"Be gone, you hag! If you don't get away from me, I'll crush you to nothing between my hands! Then you'd be no more than a spot of grease!"

Old Larisa withdrew from the angry prince; but she simply hurried through the alleys in order to confront him further along his route.

"Good day, Prince Ivan. Why are you so sad?"

Her boldness made the prince thoughtful. "Perhaps," he thinks to himself, "this old woman will be useful."

"Well, granny, I'm sad because I cannot fulfill my mission without a good steed, and I cannot fine one."

"Why, you silly fellow! Why do you suffer so, when you could ask for help from this old lady? Well, Prince, come along now."

Larisa led Prince Ivan to the top of a nearby hill and pointed to a place beyond.

"Do you see that spot of ground with the deep, green grass? You must dig there."

Following the old woman's counsel, Prince Ivan dug into the dark earth until he uncovered a heavy iron plate, secured with a dozen iron padlocks. Relying on the amazing strength in his hands, he ripped off all twelve padlocks and raised the iron plate. Within was a passage leading deep underground. He soon entered a cavernous stable in which a handsome stallion was chained. A dozen heavy chains had been holding the horse. However, when the stallion saw the approaching prince, it realized that a proper horseman was about to saddle him again; so the steed reared and twisted from side to side until every one of the twelve chains snapped.

While the impatient stallion snorted and reared, Prince Ivan glanced about the stable until he caught sight of a magnificent, beautifully tooled saddle that he quickly recognized as the work of the skilled tribesmen of Circassia near the Black Sea. The prince strapped the handsome Circassian saddle onto the horse. Then he grabbed a bridle and attached that, too. With saddle and bridle in place, Prince Ivan lifted some excellent armor from a heavy hook on the stable wall. Quickly donning the strong armor, the youngest prince led the steed to the entrance through which he had entered this underground stable.

Now grateful, Prince Ivan handed Larisa a couple of coins, saying "Forgive my lack of courtesy, Granny, and please bless me."

He mounted the powerful steed and rode away.

The prince rode for hours, until he arrived at the base of a mountain. Just as he arrived at the mountain, his two brothers rode in from another direction. His brothers told Ivan of their failed efforts to even locate their mother; much less to rescue her. "Perhaps," said Ivan, "she is being held captive on top of this mountain."

Then, the three siblings spent the daylight hours of two full days riding their horses around the base of the mountain; but they found no way to scale its high, steep sides. However, near where they were to finish their encircling ride, the brothers noticed a chunk of raw iron, weighing at least five poods [A pood is a Russian weight of 36 pounds.]. The iron rock was inscribed. All three princes dismounted and stooped to read the inscription, which said: "To him who hurls this rock against the mountain, a way to scale the mountain will be revealed."

All three brothers were eager to try hurling the rock; but the older two brothers could do little more that lift the rock from the ground. Prince Ivan, however, took a deep breath, positioned himself and raised the rock until it was above his head. He stood for a moment, steadying himself. Then he threw the iron rock against the mountainside!

From above, a thick rope ladder tumbled downward, to dangle in front of the king's sons.

Prince Ivan tethered his steed. He then withdrew a small glass vial and a dagger from the saddlebag.

He quickly punctured the small finger of his left hand and let a few drops of blood fall into the vial. He handed the vial to Illarion. Then Ivan addressed his two older brothers: "This blood will turn black if I am about to die. It that occurs, flee for your own safety." They nodded in agreement. Ivan said farewell to the two men and began climbing the ladder.

When Ivan reached the top of the mountain, he saw a magnificent plateau. It was filled with lush orchards of many varieties of fruit, as well as a huge variety of birds and natural fountains bringing forth sparkling streams. The heroic prince began following a narrow path through this mountain-plateau wonderland. After a lengthy walk, he arrived at a huge house, which was the prison in which another king's daughter, Iskra, was being held captive by the deathless Koshchei.

Prince Ivan walked around the house, seeking access to the building. There was no doorway to be seen. However, within the house, the imprisoned maiden heard Ivan's movements and stepped onto a balcony. She then told Ivan that he could come in if he pressed a hidden recess in the door frame. By doing as she had instructed, Ivan opened the huge hidden door and entered the dwelling. The princess Iskra, making no effort to escape, offered Ivan food and wine. While providing refreshment for this weary hero, the maiden also questioned him. Ivan told her that he was on a mission to rescue his mother, Inessa, who was kidnapped by Koshchei.

The maiden said that Ivan would likely be unable to rescue his mother, who was being kept in the next house to be reached by walking further along this same narrow path. Iskra felt sure that rescue was impossible, since Koshchei was truly deathless. However, she said that Koshchei often came to visit her and that a sword belonging to

Koshchei was propped against the very wall near which Ivan was seated.

"Koshchei is no mortal, you know. But, perhaps, if you are strong enough to lift that sword, you might have a chance to succeed in your rescue mission."

Ivan eagerly eyed the sword. It weighed 50 poods [Nearly a ton]! Still, his superhuman strength aided his effort. He not only lifted the sword; but he tossed it into the air! Then he thanked Iskra, the kidnapped princess, for the refreshment and for the information she had given. When he left the house, he closed the door, so that the maiden – who seemed content with her captivity - was again unable to open the door from within.

After walking briskly for another four versts [three miles], Ivan arrived at another large house. He now knew how to access the house. He quickly found the hidden chink in the door frame and released the massive door. There sat his kidnapped mother, staring at the floor and looking very sad and forlorn. He stepped into the room. His mother, Inessa, slowly looked toward Ivan.

The recognition brought a smile to the mother's face and tears to her eyes. Both mother and son wept as he held her. Then she whimpered loudly as she said that a massive iron ball was mounted in such a way that it would crush her if she tried to escape with Ivan. But, once again, Ivan looked at this challenge to his strength. His strength had never been tested like this. The iron sphere easily weighed many poods [several tons]! This required some pondering.

At that moment, Inessa jerked with fear! She sensed the arrival of Koshchei.

"Move quickly, my son! Koshchei is just beyond the doorway! Here, this fruit bin is nearly empty. Climb in here and be very quiet."

Koshchei burst into the room, quickly surveyed the entire room and then demanded,

"There's the smell of a Russian man in here! The house reeks with the smell of a Russian man. Who was here, woman? Was one of your sons here?"

The terrified woman kept her wits. She moved close to Koshchei, teasing,

"What are you talking about, Koshchei? Bless you... you've been flying about over Russia and the odor clings to your nostrils."

Moving from one topic to another, she continued, "Have you seen how full the fruit trees have become? It's time to gather the fruit. My dear Koshchei, I'll prepare you some dishes with fresh fruit. Then I'll dry and preserve the rest of the crop."

"Yes, I've seen the fruit trees sagging under the weight of their crop. But, I am too hungry to think of fruit. Where is the roasted fowl that I left when breaking fast this morning? If I was mortal, I'd be dead now from hunger!"

The ideal moment had arrived. Since her abduction, she'd been tempted to ask him this question; but had been too terrified of his anger to broach the subject.

"Koshchei, you once said that all things face death; but you've not told me where your death resides...."

"That's easy... my death resides precisely in the center of this plateau. You can see the exact spot because there is a massive oak tree at that spot. It stands taller than any other tree on the plateau. Beneath the oak there is a casket of walnut wood. Within the walnut casket there is a hare. Within the hare is a duck. Within the duck is an egg. Finally... within the egg...."

Koshchei the Deathless paused dramatically. He mouth formed into a twisted smile, reflecting his swollen pride.

Inessa twisted her head slightly, as if in wonderment. That gesture prodded Koshchei to continue.

"Within the egg... is my death!"

Here was a secret that enemies of Koshchei shouldn't know; but that was of no concern to the evil Koshchei. His abducted queen was the only one who heard his secret... except for her hidden son.

As the minutes unfolded, Koshchei tarried. Inessa feigned friendliness. Prince Ivan kept his agonizing doubled-over state within the fruit bin.

Presently, Koshchei stirred. He moved toward the fruit bin. "Well, I've deeds to do. I'll grab a ripe pear and be on my way."

"Oh, wait...wait Koshchei! The more succulent pears are in the pannier by the window... where your servant sat them this morning."

She grabbed a pear in each hand and presented them to Koshchei. His hand already on the knob that opened the fruit bin, he turned to see what she offered. They appeared to be ripe enough. He released the knob and reached for the pears that Inessa proffered. Then, holding both pears in one of his huge hands, he opened the door and, with a final glance around the room, he flew from the house. Ivan, stiff and frightened, exited the safety of the bin. He stretched his aching limbs and asked his mother for her blessing, so that he could go to find and destroy Koshchei's death. Queen Inessa pronounced her blessing on her son, handed him a bag of victuals and a warm blanket for sleeping wherever he found himself at nightfall. Then she kissed him goodbye and pulled shut the door behind him. He walked briskly along the path toward the center of the plateau.

By twilight, Prince Ivan was very fatigued and hungry. He found a sheltered spot within a copse of trees, ate the food he'd been carrying and wrapped himself in the warm blanket. He slept soundly.

At daybreak, the youngest prince was already walking along the path that led toward the center of the mountain plateau. When the pathway arrived at the top of a hill, Ivan looked far ahead, beyond a nearer lake. He could see, quite clearly, a large stand of oak trees. Standing out among them was a particularly tall oak. This, Ivan, realized, was the tree he sought.

As the undaunted youngest son of a king, Ivan strolled at a fast clip. However, he was soon very hungry. Spying a young wolf near the path, he was determined to kill it for the meat which he craved. However, a she wolf leaped from her den and addressed Ivan. "Please, don't harm my young one. I promise to do you a good turn, sometime." He accepted the promise of the mother wolf and moved on. Soon after that encounter, Ivan saw a crow perched on a low branch; an easy target. As he loaded his gun, the crow suddenly cawed, "Please, don't hurt me. I promise to do you a good turn when you need one." Although famished, Ivan decided to forego the snack in favor of the crow's promise. He trudged on, hungrier than ever.

Prince Ivan soon came to the azure waters of a deep, lake. Just then a small pike jumped from the waters and landed on the lake's shore. "Now!" exclaimed Ivan, grabbing the young pike, "I'll eat at last!" However, at that moment, an immense pike appeared on the lake's surface. "Please, Prince Ivan. Don't hurt my young. I'll surely return the favor." Again, the prince decided to forego a meal. He released the pike back into deeper water. However, this left Ivan looking for a path to travel around the lake. At that moment, the large pike swam to Ivan and offered its sturdy back. Ivan stepped onto the pike and balanced himself on its broad back. The pike swam across the lake, depositing Ivan on the far side, just a short distance from the giant oak.

Sure enough. Beneath the oak was a small casket. Ivan quickly opened it; but a hare suddenly jumped out and darted toward the thickest clump of trees! Ivan felt devastated. His chance to gain Koshchei's death had disappeared into the thicket! He cursed himself for his failure. How could he have been so reckless?

Just then a young wolf – the one that Ivan had earlier spared – came onto the scene, pursued the hare and caught it. The wolf returned the hare to Ivan. Ivan happily and eagerly cut open the hare; but was stunned when a duck jumped from the split hare and flew away! Ivan shot at the duck in flight; but without success. Once again, the prince was downcast. Once again, though, another of his good turns was rewarded. The crow that Ivan had spared suddenly appeared, with several other crows. They pursued the fleeing duck and caught it. When they returned the duck to Ivan, he cut it open and extracted the duck's egg. However, when he got to the lake he decided to wash the egg. It slipped into the water and Ivan's quick lurch failed to catch it. Ivan saw the egg sinking toward the lake bottom. It was quickly out of his reach and out of sight. He was lost! But, once again, he was aided by a recipient of his own mercy. The waters soon began churning and out popped the large pike... clutching the egg in its mouth!

Further, the pike again provided a ride for Ivan to get back across the lake. From that shore, he set a very fast pace walking, so that, by nightfall, he reached the house where his mother was confined.

After Inessa greeted her brave son, she quickly hid him, as before. Soon Koschei flew up to the house and let himself in. Again, he snorted, "Why do I smell a Russian man again? The aroma assails my sensitive nostrils!"

"Oh, Dear Koshchei. What are you talking about? There's no one else in this place!"

Just then, Koshchei, the Deathless, twisted with discomfort. "I am feeling quite ill."

Unknown to Koshchei, Prince Ivan, hiding within the fruit bin, was squeezing the egg!

Again, Ivan squeezed the egg, only harder.

Koshchei the Deathless doubled over with pain!

Suddenly, Prince Ivan emerged from the fruit bin, gripping the egg securely! He exclaimed,

"There is your death, O Koshchei the Deathless!"

Koshchei the Deathless crumpled to the floor, begging, "Don't kill me, Prince Ivan! We can be friends! All the world will lie at our feet!"

Unimpressed, the brave prince, with the egg between his powerful hands, quickly crushed it. As the pieces of egg shell dropped to the floor, Koshchei writhed in agony for a moment before collapsing in death.

Ivan and his mother gathered whatever struck their fancy, tied the loot within a large bag and moved toward the door.

"Oh! Oh! Wait, Ivan!"

Inessa recalled the giant iron ball that was part of the system of imprisonment she had known since her abduction. She reminded Ivan of the deadly trap that Koshchei had rigged so that she could never escape. Koshchei's curse still held the ball. Both Inessa and Ivan realized that the massive ball, which did not fall when Koshchei or Ivan used the doorway, was under a spell by Koshchei and was only fall when Inessa attempted to leave. Ivan was tempted to try lifting the huge, heavy sphere; but studied the frame of heavy timbers that held the ball, ready to drop during that moment when Inessa stepped into the doorway! He looked about the room. There beside the stove stood a great ax, used for cutting firewood. A normal man could not have lifted the great ax; but Ivan not only lifted the large ax; but he swung it mightily against the frame that held the giant ball.

The wooden beam, cut through by Ivan's mighty swing of the ax, collapsed. Both Inessa and Ivan leaped away from the crunching and crumbling frame. As they watched, the massive iron ball dropped. It crashed through the heavy oaken floor boards and plunged into the basement beneath.

Ivan lifted his mother across the gaping, broken floor boards and then he, too, leaped across. Inessa was liberated at last.

As the mother and son – queen and prince – walked to the edge of the plateau, they came to the house where the princess, Iskra, was a captive. Ivan promptly released her and the three strode toward the ladder, the only means of getting off the mountain. As they walked, Ivan told his mother how kindly he had been treated by Iskra. As the three spoke, it became clear that Princess Iskra and Prince Ivan wanted to marry when they reached his father's kingdom. Inessa was enthusiastic with her blessing of the attractive couple.

As they reached the ladder, below which the other two princes were waiting, Iskra suddenly remembered something that she prized. She asked Ivan if he would please return to the house where she had been imprisoned. There, she said, Ivan would find her marriage robe, her diamond ring and a pair of seamless shoes. [In an earlier century, only costly shoes were made without seams where the leather was sown together.] Ivan sent the two women down the ladder while he returned to the house to retrieve Iskra's prized possessions.

The older brothers had been scheming. When the women reached the ground, the middle brother, Veniamin, climbed to the very top of the ladder and cut it partially through. He climbed down again, as gingerly and cautiously as he could. Then the two conspiring brothers tugged and tugged until the rope ladder snapped and fell into a heap at their feet.

The women were aghast. They protested loudly; but the two princes made the most vile threats against the two women, if even one word was spoken about the incident when they reached the kingdom of King Pavel. When the quartet reached the home kingdom, King Pavel was thrilled to see his wife and two older sons had survived; but grieved mightily for his lost son, Ivan.

Prince Ivan, carrying the treasures of his intended wife came, once again, to the cliff. Here, he discovered the flimsy remains of the crucial ladder and guessed what had happened. While pondering his seemingly impossible situation, he tossed the wedding ring from hand to hand. Suddenly, a dozen strong, young men appeared. Quickly guessing that the ring was enchanted, he told the young men that he needed a way to get off the mountain. They clung, hands to feet, and formed a ladder, which Ivan used to get to the bottom of the mountain. When he dropped to the solid ground from the last young man's feet, he slipped the enchanted ring onto his small finger... and the young men disappeared.

The betrayed prince returned to his native city. He sought lodging with the old woman, Larisa, who had befriended him before. He soon asked her, "What news do you have of the land?"

"The news, Prince, is woeful to hear. Your two brothers have returned, bringing along your mother, the queen, and a beautiful princess from another land. The bothers told your grieving father, the king, that you had perished. Now, then, Prince Illarion has said that he plans to marry the beautiful princess. He also insisted on a quick wedding; but the princess said that she won't marry until he gets her betrothal ring or until he gets one made just like it, from her description. Prince Illarion has been trying and trying to find someone who can make just such a ring. He is offering a handsome sum to the person who can fashion such a ring."

Prince Ivan was delighted. "Well, Granny, go tell the king that you will make one. I'll see that you have one to give!"

Larisa put on the finest articles of clothing from her shoddy wardrobe and, although very nervous, went to see King Pavel.

"Please, your Majesty. I can make such an engagement ring."

"Make it, mother, make it!" the king said, adding, "I welcome your offer; but remember... if you don't make it, off goes your head."

Larisa, trembling and sobbing, returned home to relay the king's dire warning. Ivan only laughed.

"Why do you laugh?" Larisa chided, "You're not in this scrape. I am. I was such a fool!"

The old woman sat in her old chair and cried herself to sleep. Ivan also slept.

Early in the morning, Ivan awakened the old lady and showed her Iskra's ring. "Remember," Ivan cautioned, say nothing about me. Tell them that you made it yourself. Also, take no more than a single ducat as your reward!"

Old Larisa was thrilled. She hurried away with the ring. Princess Iskra was amazed at the ring's beauty and, it seemed, its perfect duplication. Then they offered old Larisa a dish full of gold. She reached into the dish and lifted out just one ducat.

"Why do you take so little? asked King Pavel.

"What good would it do? If I need more, you can offer again."

The old lady left and it was soon rumored that the Princess Iskra had made a similar request regarding the wedding dress. The princess wanted her own wedding dress or one exactly like it. Again, Larisa presented the perfect dress, claiming that she had sewn it herself. Then she soon had the opportunity to present the princess with a pair of seamless shoes that were exactly as Princess Iskra had requested. Each time, Larisa accepted a single ducat from the amount offered. Each time Larisa had presented the objects that Prince Ivan had secretly presented to her. Prince Ivan then asked the old woman to tell him, as soon as she learned of the exact time and place for the wedding between Princess Iskra and the treacherous Prince Illarion.

Now the king announced that the glorious event was to be held on the next holy day. The kingdom felt the excitement and Prince Ivan felt a scheme developing. When old Larisa told him of the precise time for the ceremony, Prince Ivan quickly donned his princely clothing. Dressed, thusly, the prince told the old woman, "This is the real me!"

Old Larisa promptly fell at his feet. "I pray that you will forgive me for scolding you," she muttered.

Prince Ivan answered her with a reassuring phrase, "God be with you."

Prince Ivan walked to the church and checked within. The bride was awaiting Illarion's arrival. When Prince Ivan saw that his brothers were not yet arrived, he strode into the church and stood by Iskra. With the Prince's prodding, the ceremony was hastily performed and he and Iskra were declared to be married.

As they were being escorted back to the palace, Prince Illarion met them. Realizing what had happened, Prince Illarion, the shamed, would-be groom, quickly left the scene.

King Pavel and Queen Inessa were thrilled to see that Prince Ivan was safe and was now married to the charming Princess Iskra. The queen was now free to explain the treachery of Illarion and Veniamin. By the time that the wedding feast was eaten, King Pavel had made a royal decision. The two older princes were banished from the kingdom and the king named Prince Ivan as the official heir to the throne. By the time the dishonored princes crossed the border into exile, the entire kingdom had heard of the exploits of Prince Ivan, the hero who had outmaneuvered the conspiratorial older brothers and had overcome and destroyed the wicked Koshchei the Deathless.

FROST!

Educators' Complement

Student Challenge,
For Greater Depth

INTRODUCTION

This section of *FROST!* offers study challenges for each skazka or folk tale appearing in this book. The challenges are divided into three parts: The Vintage Vocabulary, the General Vocabulary, and Three Essayettes. All work is this section is designed to require some thought on the part of the reader. All should improve the reader's word, writing and thinking skills. The reader is expected to recall and to analyze what has been read in each skazka.

Before undertaking the student challenge, a trio of simple writing objectives are suggested. Think about them. After all, whether this book is being used for its cultural value or its literary worth, your written responses should reveal a concern for effective writing.

A. *Reflect on the logic of your sentences.* Here are three examples:

1. "so that sparks fell onto flammable material such as the bark from certain trees the Indians carried with them."
   John L. Moore, *The Daily Item* (Sunbury, PA), 3/25/1, p.B4

Do the words of that sentence need to be rearranged in order to omit the comical picture of Indians struggling under the weight of the trees that they are carrying across the frontier landscape?

2. "The North Platte is one of those rare streams that runs north."
   Mort Künstler, *Mort Künstlers Old West: Cowboys,* Nashville, TN, 1998, p. 174

This statement is wrong. **Streams that flow north are not rare!** That is a misconception. Simply check any map of North America, Siberia, Hawaii, Australia, etc., for northward-flowing rivers. Streams simply flow downhill (with gravity), **in all directions!**

3. "A woman who must have been a model removed a bottle from her purse. She raised it high and squirted a long stream down onto her cupped hands."
   Joel Stein, *TIME*, 3/15/00
Here the writer has carelessly created a picture that either confuses or amuses?

B. *Write your first draft with simple, short words.* Short words are as respectable as larger ones. Use larger words, as needed, for variety or when a more precise meaning is helpful. Here are two examples: You or I might write: *Person Who Is the Object of the Intermittent Sounding of A Resonant Metal Dome*, while Ernest Hemingway simply said, *For Whom the Bell Tolls*. Also, you or I might write, *The Beautifully Luminescent, Sand-induced Sphere*, while John Steinbeck wrote simply, *The Pearl*.

C. *Avoid mutant modifiers.*
A 'mutant modifier' is simply this author's phrase for identifying superfluous modifiers that are foolishly attached to verbs. Such errant modifiers were recognized, and condemned, for at least the past one and one-half centuries and many of the best writers rarely use them. Other writers use them carelessly and often. Let's begin with a sentence whose writer jammed a modifier into a perfectly fine and clear sentence. He hobbles a very robust verb with a burdensome modifier:

"In an effort to bolster **up** the confession...."
   Ralph Roeder, The Man of the Renaissance,
   TIME Reading Program, Special Edition, 1966, p. 121.

In the above example, the word 'up' has no role and should not be present. The word 'bolster' is clear and effective alone. Try to spot the worthless modifier in the following dozen quotes:

1. "cause the loosely connected bones of the skull to spread apart...."
   Mike Durso, www.franktenaglia.com/padrepio

2. "We've trimmed down our unlimited calling plan."
   Envelope blurb from a Verizon mailing, received during May of 2006.

3. The justiciar... had gathered up his records and documents and taken flight."
   Thomas B. Costain, *The Three Edwards*, Garden City, New York, 1958 & 1962, p. 63.

4. "How do you soften up militants...."
   Lisa Beyer, *TIME*, 8/7/06, p. 27.

5. "an occasion on which he met up with the tenor...."
   Armando Cesari, *Mario Lanza: An American Tragedy*, p. 61.

6. "He would not tell investigators where he had been hiding out...."
   Ken Ritter, A.P., *The Daily Item*, 8/30/06, p. A2.

7. "To back up his photographs...."
   Elizabeth Winthrop, *Smithsonian*, 9/06, p. 20.

8. "the shack where we had slept and worked was sealed off as police conducted forensic studies."
   Jeff Israely, *TIME*, 4/24/06, p. 45.

9. "a small blond man, laden down with musical instruments...."
   Helen L. Kaufmann, *The Little Book of Music Anecdotes*, New York, 1948, p. 254.

10. "Grades are rounded off to the nearest whole percentage...."
   THE E-Z GRADER © 1994, B. C. Richards.

11. "Some of the biggest names in entertainment join together to raise awareness...."
   J.C. Penny ad, *The Daily Item*, 8/21/06, p. A5.

12. We all know how that's worked out."
   The Week, 5/26/06, p. 14.

One can't imagine the fictional spy, James Bond, being offered a mixed drink and requesting that it be "Shaken **up**; not stirred **up**." Nor can we imagine William Shakespeare writing, "All's well that ends **up** well." Neither James Bond's creator nor William Shakespeare used mutant modifiers in these two critical bits of writing; nor should **we**.

You should have found one mutant modifier in each of the dozen examples. Think about them as you write. Without them, your writing will have greater crispness and clarity. Now, let's get down to business... and remember to write your answers, etc., on separate paper.

Ilya and the Wolf Pack

For both the vintage (older, almost unused) terms and the general vocabulary, write the word and, using a dictionary definition, use the word in a fresh, clear sentence.

Vintage Vocabulary: *vintage, flask*

General Vocabulary: *lupine, ascend*

Essayettes: Choose any one of the following three topics and write a brief essay (according to your instructor's specifications) around the chosen topic.

1. Discuss how Ilya's fortunes changed because of his kindness and mention how these benefits happened.
2. List and discuss the few real facts that are given relating to trapping for fur pelts as Ilya does.
3. Analyze all the events that match for both Ilya and his brother Leonid. This similarity is used to make the story more interesting.

The One-eyed Demon

Vintage Vocabulary: *anvil, shepherd's crook, awl, hapless, warren*

General Vocabulary: *demon, sylvan, wane, cowered, taunted, gait, wrath, enchantment, stench, desperation, harrowing, ordeal*

Essayettes: Choose any one of the following three topics and write a brief essay (according to your instructor's specifications) around the chosen topic.

1. What is this skazka's most bizarre aspect? Explain what makes that part of the tale seem to be bizarre.
2. Decide and discuss what impression the narrator apparently wants to leave with the reader as a lesson to be learned.
3.   Select and write the phrase in which the writer tells why it is impossible for Feodor to remove either his hand or the golden axe. Mention how the writer lists the ever-increasing forces that hold the axe.

The Midnight Visitor

Vintage Vocabulary: *crock, latch*

General Vocabulary: *envy, widower, cradle, ghastly*

Essayettes: Choose any one of the following three topics and write a brief essay (according to your instructor's specifications) around the chosen topic.

1. Describe the evidence of strange behavior by the newborn that was seen by its elderly caretaker. Why was the infant acting so strangely?
2. Relate which events in this folk tale are utterly unscientific and what makes them so.
3. Describe the various aspects of village life that the reader can learn from this folk tale.

Crossing the Don

Vintage Vocabulary: *tsar, kopeck*

General Vocabulary: *ford, surname, sonorous, suppliant, destination, inducted, imperial, rivulet, daunting, furlough, respite, incessant, undercurrent, canteen*

Essayettes: Choose any one of the following three topics and write a brief essay (according to your instructor's specifications) around the chosen topic.

1. Discuss the initial business between Oleg and the Don, telling which purchased what.
2. Carefully describe the progress of Oleg's boasting of his favored treatment by the Don River.
3. Explain what changed the attitudes of both Oleg and the Don River as the story progressed.

The Headless Princess

Vintage Vocabulary: *sideboard, samovar, deviltry, malady, chaff*

General Vocabulary: *tutor, mosey, engrossed, primping, grieving, apprehension, wizened, tremble, perplexed, agitate, vale, ghoulish, thunderclap, suppliant, harrowing, disheveled*

Essayettes: Choose any one of the following three topics and write a brief essay (according to your instructor's specifications) around the chosen topic.

1. What role does Alexey's tutor play in this skazka? Explain her role and how she wants to save Alexey, telling what evidence reveals how much she wants him to survive.
2. Describe the king's sorry role in this tale, from the point of his daughter's strange request until her actual death.
3. Analyze the three most terrifying horrors witnessed by Alexey and tell which is the very worst

and what makes it the worst. What character traits does Alexey exhibit throughout the story?

Frost

Vintage Vocabulary: *dote, lazybones, ruble, greybeard, sledge, greatcoat, wretch*

General Vocabulary: *obstinate, samovar, connive, stiff-necked*

Essayettes: Choose any one of the following three topics and write a brief essay (according to your instructor's specifications) around the chosen topic.

1. Compare this girl's ordeal with that of the famous Cinderella. What are the major differences and the major similarities (include the family situations, evidence or lack of evidence for wealth, their marriages, etc.   2. Explain your impression of Maxim, so far as his reaction to his wife and to the way that he changes his approach to her with the death of her two daughters.
3. Contrast the behavior of both Marfa and her two sisters when forced to suffer from the increasing cold.

Ivashko

Vintage Vocabulary: *girdling, hobbled, wailing, jubilant*

General Vocabulary: *assurance, hoarse, crimson, rant, tremble, imploring*

Essayettes: Choose any one of the following three topics and write a brief essay (according to your instructor's specifications) around the chosen topic.

1. Describe what you feel to be the most bizarre development in this folk tale and what makes it seem to be so strange.
2. Compare the similarities between this story and the story of Hansel and Gretel.
3. Discuss the use of repetition in this story, in the spoken statements that are repeated and in events that occur two or more times. Does such repetition make the story seem more old fashioned or less old fashioned? Does it, or does it not, help to build tension?

Two Comrades

Vintage Vocabulary: *saddler, churchyard, Maker, spectral, score (of years), dumbfounded*

General Vocabulary: *carousing, reins, declaration, dutiful, forlorn, transfixed, elude, anxiety, nave, alcove, abject*

Essayettes: Choose any one of the following three topics and write a brief essay (according to your instructor's specifications) around the chosen topic.

1. Compare this skazka with the version written and made famous by Washington Irving, the Rip Van Winkle story. What aspects of the two tales are similar or the same? What are the major differences in the tales?
2. Explain how the writer described the results of the cemetery's sixty years of aging.

3. Tell what the writer describes that would add to Anton's growing anxiety, from the time the grave falls shut until he learns what happened to his planned wedding ceremony.

Lukan's Ladder

Vintage Vocabulary: *shabby, cackling, hovel, mead, savory, succulent, glut, canister, cottager*

General Vocabulary: *solitary, impoverished, cram, moocher, mired, immobile, dilapidated*

Essayettes: Choose any one of the following three topics and write a brief essay (according to your instructor's specifications) around the chosen topic.

1. Compare the story of Lukan with that of Jack and the Beanstalk. Explain the similarities and the differences.
2. Develop a profile of Lukan's behavior while up in the clouds. Let your profile reveal the very human weaknesses that Lukan displayed from his arrival until his climb down his trusty rope.
3. Show, in written form, the examples in this skazka of Lukan having several things occur that any poor man might wish would happen.

The Steed and the Stone

Vintage Vocabulary: *farrier, steed*

General Vocabulary: *addled*

Essayettes: Choose any one of the following three topics and write a brief essay (according to your instructor's specifications) around the chosen topic.
1. Explain why Boris might have found himself clinging to a tombstone.
2. Identify and discuss the strange situation between Boris and his friend, Vassili.
3. Offer opinions about why there are graveyards involved in many folk tales.

The Fiddler in Hell

Vintage Vocabulary: *nettles, flailed, hank catgut*

General Vocabulary: *fiends, gibberish, sarcastically, thrift*

Essayettes: Choose any one of the following three topics and write a brief essay (according to your instructor's specifications) around the chosen topic.

1. Explain the events that lead the fiddler to realize that he had fiddled at Konstantin's funeral.
2. Discuss the situation that put Konstantin in the lowest depth of hell.
3. Select which individual was the main character of this folk tale and explain your selection.

Sozh and Dnieper

Vintage Vocabulary: *liveryman, spendthrift, besotted*

General Vocabulary: *conspire, fume, tributary, sibling, riverine*

Essayettes: Choose any one of the following three topics and write a brief essay (according to your instructor's specifications) around the chosen topic.

1. Research the Biblical tale of Jacob and Esau and identify the similarities that you find between this skazka and the Jacob/Esau account.
2. Identify the two birds mentioned in this skazka and explain the role of each.
3. Relate how the closing paragraph slips from fantasy into geographical fact. Mention the lone, six-letter word in that paragraph that suggests a human characteristic.

The Shroud

Vintage Vocabulary: *lazybones, sweetmeats, distaff, askance, shroud, pilfer*

General Vocabulary: *icon, sacrilege, cleft, despair, impasse, dilemma*

Essayettes: Choose any one of the following three topics and write a brief essay (according to your instructor's specifications) around the chosen topic.

1. Explain why the challenge to Veronika's boasting is doubling dangerous in the girls' minds.
2. Discuss how the behavior of the corpse suggests that the corpse was rather calm.
3. Decide whether or not you think the fate of Veronika was too severe. Explain your choice.

The Warrior and the Warlock

Vintage Vocabulary: *reminisced, rouble (also spelled ruble), vial, pyre, cooperage*

General Vocabulary: *miserly, isolation, bravado, draft (animal), envelop, grimace, domain, unique, cringed, jeopardy, residue, diligent, speculation, calamity, incredulous*

Essayettes: Choose any one of the following three topics and write a brief essay (according to your instructor's specifications) around the chosen topic.

1. Identify the several times that the dead warlock insults Timofey and suggest why it makes the conclusion to the story more satisfying to the reader.
2. List the several things done by Timofey that suggest his perfection as an heroic individual.
3. Describe the most bizarre part of this folk tale and explain your choice.

Mother Friday

Vintage Vocabulary: forsooth, taper

General Vocabulary: wretch

Essayettes:

1. Explain how you suppose such a tradition as the Mother Friday tradition might have begun. You might mention the obvious discomfort created by the dust involved in their work.
2. Compare the behavior of Raisa with that of the

other women who were present. 3.
3. Discuss the two promises that Raisa makes to
Mother Friday.

The Witch of Death

Vintage Vocabulary: dumbfounded

General Vocabulary: whimper, constable, sexton

Essayettes:

1. What attributes did Emelian possess that
prepared him to be a hero?
2. Identify the steps involved in recognizing who,
among the villagers, was a witch.
3. What titles were held by local laws officials?

The Two Corpses

Vintage Vocabulary: ghastly, churchyard

General Vocabulary: devoid, mortal, simpering,
ravenous

Essayettes:

1. Describe how the soldier came to be inside the
small chapel.
2. Discuss the arguments of the two hungry
corpses.
3. Analyze the reaction of the soldier, relating to
his bravery or lack of it.

The Woodland Damsel

Vintage Vocabulary: trice, nimrod, rouble, rill

General Vocabulary: quarry, terrain, livelihood, siblings

Essayettes:

1. Discuss the evidence that Oksana became somewhat acclimated to the forest.
2. Analyze the information that suggests that Rodion was an able hunter.
3. Identify the role of Sirius in this story.

The Blind Man and the Cripple

Vintage Vocabulary: wrought, boyar, quartered, compatriot

General Vocabulary: consulted, riddler, haughty, thwarting, stranded, spouse, dissuade

Essayettes:

1. Describe the several things that reveal the similarity between "The Immortal Koshchei" and the opera plot for "Turandot."
2. Offer your own opnion regarding the great transformation of Princess Anna's personality at the close of the skazka.
3. List the supernatural happenings that you feel clearly indicate that this is a fairy tale or folk tale.

The Immortal Koschei

There are many versions of the Koshchei character throughout Eurasia. This one was based on one of the more popular versions.

Vintage Vocabulary: hag, forlorn, pannier, ducat

General Vocabulary: grotesque, immortality, appendage, tether, exile

Essayettes: (open with such words as discuss, explain, compare, analyze, etc.)

1. Discuss how the Koshchei could be overcome and killed. Express your own opinion: Is the tale more, or less, appealing because the Koshchei has so few vulnerabilities? Discuss.
2. Folk tales that are familiar to Americans have fairy godmothers. In this tale, what would be the nearest equivalent to a fairy godmother? Discuss the characteristics. Cite an example of the old lady's sharp verbal response.
3. Discuss the once-common practice, in many nations, of always making the oldest son of a ruler the heir to the throne? Compare the advantages and disadvantages of such a practice. Compare the three sons of this tale in formulating your answer.

CONCLUSION

As this book suggests, Russian folk tales are varied and numerous. The reader should also be aware that Russian history is very old and very rich. The Russians have given the world many great literary and musical works. Students might begin to reach into Russia's rich cultural treasure chest by compiling a list, with brief biographies, of the nation's tsars, or political leaders, or prominent women, or composers, or writers or sports figures. One might also study its great heritage of architecture or its near-endless geography. No matter how much you, as an individual, delve into Russia's national heritage, we thank you for joining us in reading some of their many skazkas.